Carl Weber Presents:

Ride or Die Chick 3

Carl Weber Presents:

Ride or Die Chick 3

J.M. Benjamin

www.urbanbooks.net

Urban Books, LLC
97 N 18th Street
Wyandanch, NY 11798

Carl Weber Presents Ride or Die Chick 3
Copyright © 2015 J.M. Benjamin

ISBN 13: 978-1-60162-649-3
ISBN 10: 1-60162-649-5

First Trade Paperback Printing March 2015
Printed in the United States of America

10 9 8 7 6 5 4 3 2 1

*This is a work of fiction. Any references or similarities
to actual events, real people, living, or dead, or to real
locales are intended to give the novel a sense of reality.
Any similarity in other names, characters, places, and
incidents is entirely coincidental.*

Distributed by Kensington Publishing Corp.
Submit Orders to:
Customer Service
400 Hahn Road
Westminster, MD 21157-4627
Phone: 1-800-733-3000
Fax: 1-800-659-2436

Carl Weber Presents:
Ride or Die Chick 3

by

J.M. Benjamin

Also by J.M. Benjamin

Down In The Dirty
Ride or Die Chick
Ride or Die Chick 2
Ride or Die Chick 3
On The Run With Love
From Incarceration 2 Incorporation
Heaven & Earth
My Manz And 'Em (Revised Edition)
Memoirs Of An Accidental Hustler
Soft (An Anthology)
Menace II Society (Anthology)
Christmas In The Hood (Anthology)

Dedication

This book is dedicated to all the many supporters who have rode for me continuously throughout the past and recent years.

The moment you stop riding will be the moment I put down my pen!

This book is also dedicated to ALL the Independent Authors/Publishers who ride for themselves and continue to make their presence felt in this competitive literary world. To you I say, keep making yourselves relevant and continue to be the Bosses that you are because contrary to what's been said or what others think, hard work does pay off!

J.M. Benjamin

Prologue

"So, today's the big day, huh, Chief?" Officer Boatright asked as he brought his hand down on Chief Randle's shoulder and applied pressure.

"And what day might that be?" the chief asked dryly, never taking his eyes off his computer monitor.

"Come on, Chief. Admit it. You're excited about retiring. No more staying up late, solving crime, chasing bad guys, kicking ass and taking names. Not to mention, eating stale donuts and drinking bad coffee on the go." Officer Boatright laughed at his own humor.

Chief Randle's fingers came to a halt on the keypad and mouse. He spun around in his chair and put his hands behind his head. "If you really want to know, Boatright, no, I'm not going to miss all of the excitement that goes on around here and in this city. And, yes, I'm actually looking forward to quiet days on my boat, fishing and tossing back a couple of shots and brews. I've busted my hump long enough on this force. Now, it's time to pass the torch to one of you guys with no life, so I can start living mine." With that said, Chief Randle returned to what he had been doing prior to the officer's interruption.

"Come on, Chief. I was just joking," Officer Boatright chimed. "You can't be serious. I mean, everyone knows how much you love your work. You mean to tell me there's nothing you're going to miss?" Officer Boatright asked.

"As a matter of fact, there is." There was a brief pause. "The stale donuts and bad coffee. Now, get out of here, so I can finish up here." Chief Randle spun his chair back around.

Officer Boatright couldn't help but let out a chuckle. "That was a good one, Chief, but, if you're not going to miss all of this, then why are you still reading up on that old case on your last day, a case that is already closed and buried?"

Officer Boatright refused to let it go. He had no way of knowing his words would spark something. Chief Randle spun around for the second time like Linda Blair's head in *The Exorcist*.

"Mind your goddamn business and get the hell out of here!" the chief boomed.

The officer's eyes widened, but he was not in the least bit shocked by the chief's words or tone. Everyone knew how much of a hard ass he could be at times, but the officer did not know what he had said to cause the chief's outburst.

"Chief, whatever I said, I'm sorry," Officer Boatright apologized as he backed away from Chief Randle's desk.

Chief Randle excused him with the wave of a hand. Once he was alone, he dug into the inside pocket of his jacket and retrieved his prescription anxiety pills. He popped the top, dumped two in his hand, and tossed them into his mouth. He chased them down with a cup of cold Dunkin' Donuts coffee, which had been sitting for most of the morning.

Ever since the "suicide by cop" incident had occurred, he had been having nightmares and anxiety attacks. Images of the scene invaded his dreams regularly and were the cause of many sleepless nights. He had played the tape back a million times in his head, wondering whether something could have been done differently to prevent the tragic ending.

In all of his years as a cop, he had never experienced or witnessed anything like the situation that day on Highway 264. It amazed him that a mother could threaten to kill her own child and actually go through with it. He had been in the presence of some of the most hardened criminals in the State of Virginia and could recognize the menacing look in their eyes on site. That was why he had made the decision he had that day. Chief Randle had learned many years ago that he could learn a lot from a person's eyes. The coldhearted eyes of Teflon Jackson and the innocence in her son's eyes were what convinced Chief Randle to pull the trigger that day. He knew she meant business and knew he had to make a decision before she did.

It was that same pair of murderous eyes that had been staring him in the face in his dreams ever since. Chief Randle could still see her body sprawled out on the highway's pavement, wide-eyed and staring into his soul. Even when he thought he could shake that one set of eyes and reason with himself that he had done the right thing, it was the second pair that created the most damage. Chief Randle could never forget the way the young kid had looked up at him with tearful eyes as he laid across his mother's chest. Chief Randle had offered all he could that day, but he knew that it was not enough. He had put himself in the kid's shoes and knew it would not have been enough for him either. Chief Randle remembered how shocked the kid appeared as the paramedics detached him from his deceased mother. He also remembered how the look of shock turned into something more and how the young kid's eyes transformed from a soft brown to a hard black as he made one last attempt to comfort the boy.

"You killed my mother. I won't ever forget you," the boy had said.

The words had echoed in the chief's mind and haunted him in his sleep since the whole ordeal had transpired. Nearly two years had passed now, and, after retracing every step and combing over every inch of the case, he was finally confident that he had not been in error. He was now able to believe it when he said that if he had to do it all over again, there was nothing he would have done differently.

Chief Randle clicked his mouse and closed out the file titled **Gangster Mom's Death by Cop**. Then, he scooped up the disarrayed papers on his desk and shoved them into the trash can.

"Good riddance!" he mumbled. It was if as though a ton of weight had been lifted off his shoulders. He was relieved to be done with his own personal investigation of himself. He had to be sure he had done everything by the book.

"Now, no more nightmares," he said aloud to himself.

Chief Randle stood up and grabbed his belongings. Then, he made his final exit from the Norfolk precinct.

Chapter 1

"Good afternoon, sir. May I help you?" the white bank teller said, flashing her million dollar smile. Her name tag announced that her name was Christina.

"Yes, I would like to make a withdrawal," the dapper man answered as he placed his briefcase on the counter. He was well groomed and wore a black suit and tie.

Christina Kawoski couldn't help but notice how neatly the black gentleman's beard and mustache were trimmed. Almost to the point of being fake, she thought.

"Sure. Okay, I can help you with that. I assume you have an account here with us, so how much would you like?" Her smile was still plastered across her face. She briefly lowered her gaze to avoid staring at the customer. Had she paid closer attention, things might have turned out differently.

"I want it all, bitch!" the customer turned bank robber growled.

His words immediately drew Christina's attention back to him. Her eyes nearly shot out of her head at the sight of the gun he was brandishing. "Please, don't shoot," she stuttered. "I have a two-year-old," she added as she instinctively threw up her hands.

"Put your fuckin' hands down!" the robber snarled.

A nervous twenty-two-year-old Christina Kawoski did as she was told, and quickly lowered her hands.

"Now, fill this mu'fuckin' briefcase up with nothing but hundreds," he instructed, while cautiously looking from *left to right. Convinced that neither bank teller on either side of her had any clue as to what was taking place, the robber refocused his attention on Christina. He had returned his attention to her just in time. Before Christina Kawoski could change her mind regarding the foolish decision she had made, her thoughts were forcefully blown out of her head by the robber's .50-caliber Desert Eagle and sprayed all over the elderly female bank teller's face who stood to the right of her. The elderly teller screamed hysterically. Her screams were instantly silenced by the next shot.*

At that point, the entire bank was in a frenzied uproar. Sensing imminent danger, the security guard reached for his service revolver, but he never got to pull it. Instead, he heard the sound of a pistol being cocked right before the back of his head split open from the impact of the shot that was delivered to it from a .357 snub-nosed. The robber's partner had wasted no time backing him up. The security guard never noticed the woman dressed in all-black Islamic attire, but she had been eyeing his every move from the moment she and her partner entered the bank.

"Everybody! Down on the floor! Now!"

The male robber had drawn a second weapon and pointed it in the direction of other customers and workers while locking his first weapon on the last teller behind the counter.

"You got two choices. You can be smart and live or be a stupid hero and die," he told the black bank teller who was on the left of the deceased Christina Kawoski. If he'd had any plans on pushing the silent alarm underneath the counter, they were immediately changed after hearing the choices given to him by the robber.

"It's not your money, and it's insured," the robber added.

The teller threw his hands up in the air and backed away from the counter.

"Good choice. Now, I need you to come over here and fill this briefcase up with all hundreds," the robber instructed.

The bank teller nervously made his way over to where his dead colleague once stood.

"Now, as an extra precaution, just in case you decide to change your mind like your friend lying down there, I'm going to press this gun up against your temple as a reminder, you understand?"

The bank teller nodded.

"Babe, three more minutes," the robber's partner informed him.

"You heard the lady. Three more minutes. That means you only got one and a half before I blow your brains out and finish your job."

The robber's words were all the motivation the bank teller needed to speed up. In under a minute, the briefcase was filled to capacity with hundred dollar bills.

"Now, come around and lie over there with the rest of them." The robber waved his gun, and the teller did as he was told.

"Thank you, everyone, for your cooperation. If you want to live, I advise you to stay down until help arrives."

The robber calmly glided past the bodies that covered the floor, making his way over to the entrance of the bank, where his partner stood. As he walked with the briefcase in his hand, he heard one of the female hostages utter something but couldn't quite make out what the woman had said. Apparently, his partner had because she rushed over to the woman and grabbed her by her hair.

"Stand up, bitch!"

The female robber yanked the white woman up and onto her feet. The woman groaned in agony from the death grip the female robber had on her hair.

"Repeat that shit you just said," she ordered.

It was as though her words had fallen on deaf ears because the white woman said nothing.

"Bitch, I said repeat that shit!" The robber shoved her gun into the woman's mouth and pried it open with the barrel of the weapon. The white woman gagged and uttered something that was inaudible.

The robber removed her gun and asked, "Now, what did you say?"

"I said, 'Fucking niggers,'" she repeated dryly.

"That's what I thought you said."

The roar from the point-blank shot sent terrifying chills through all who witnessed the coldblooded act. Men, women, and children cringed with fear, hoping they would not be next.

"Do we have any more racist muthafuckas who would like to speak up?" she asked sarcastically.

There were no replies. Her partner shook his head as he thought of the monster he had created in his lover. "Babe, let's go," he said as he held the door open for her.

Then, he faced the horrified hostages and said, "Thank you again."

He turned around just in time to witness his lover's body being cut down as she was met with a barrage of bullets that found a resting place in her chest. Before he had time to react, a bullet from a sniper's gun slammed into his skull, causing him to tumble back into the bank. His body went crashing to the floor.

"No!" young Treacherous Freeman Jr. screamed as he woke up in a cold sweat.

Another bad dream about his parents had been the cause of yet another rude awakening. The other kids who shared a room with Treacherous were used to his nightmares and knew to say nothing. Many of them were afraid of him, so, even if they wanted to say something, they wouldn't. Ever since he had come to the group home, he had been having bad dreams. None of the dreams were ever the same but always ended the same and seemed so real. The end results were always that his parents were gunned down.

Almost three years had gone by, and young Treacherous still could not escape the recurring nightmares. The bad dreams remained fresh in his young mind. Ironically, after each nightmare, young Treacherous always found relief by going back to read something about his parents in one of his mother's journals he was allowed to keep after her tragic death. At that point, he had read his mother's journals so many times that he knew by heart what was on each page.

Treacherous reached under his mattress and retrieved one of them. After the last nightmare, he finished reading the words of his mother's final account of her and his father. Whenever he finished, he would always start reading from the beginning again. Although he could nearly recite the words on the pages, he continued to read because he always felt a connection to his parents whenever he read his mother's words in her own handwriting. Treacherous cracked open one of the notebooks and read until he couldn't read anymore.

Chapter 2

Fifteen-year-old Treacherous Freeman Jr. awoke to the sound of the birds chirping outside the window of his bedroom in the group home's attic. His bed was located near the window. As usual, he had dozed off while reading about his parents. It was not a surprise to him that he had the journal clenched close to his chest when he opened his eyes. Treacherous slid the journal underneath his mattress and climbed out of bed. He kneeled beside his bed, folded his hands together, and began his day the way he normally did, by talking to his parents.

"Good morning, Mom and Dad. I couldn't sleep last night. I had another bad dream about you. Like the rest of them, it seemed real, but I knew it wasn't. Y'all were dressed in disguises this time and almost got away, but, Mom, instead of Daddy losing his temper, in this one, it was you. Some lady made a racist remark, and you taught her a lesson. I think, if you would've just left, y'all would've made it out of there and it wouldn't have been a nightmare. The police were waiting for y'all out front, and they started shooting, and, Mom, you got shot up, and so did you, Dad. That's when I woke up. It didn't scare me because I'm used to it, but it made me mad because I wanted y'all to get away.

"I think about y'all all the time, especially you, Mom, and the last time I saw you. I can't stop thinking about that policeman who took you from me. If it weren't for him, you would still be here, and I wouldn't be in here.

When I get out of here, I'm going to find him, if it's the last thing I do.

"I hate this place. I hate the way they treat me here, like I'm some retard, and I hate the way they tell me what to do. I'm not going to be here too much longer, though. I have a plan. I promise I won't do anything without letting y'all know first. I just wanted to tell you about my nightmare, but, like always, Mom, after I read one of your journals, I felt better, and I fell asleep. They be wanting me to read these history books, but I'd rather read the history of y'all. I can't wait to leave Richmond and go over to the Seven Cities where you guys and my granddad were from. Well, that's it for now. I'll talk to you later. I love you both."

Everyone was still sound asleep when Treacherous finished his morning talk with his parents. Afterward, he wasted no time breaking into a pushup. After the completion of his first set, Treacherous reached for the pen and paper lying on the nightstand next to his bed and wrote down the forty-rep set. Exercising was one of the few things Treacherous enjoyed doing at the group home. What had started out as recreation for him wound up becoming a part of his daily morning routine. Within the past thirty months or so, Treacherous had gone from a puny twelve-year-old to a well-built teenager. Judging from the way his mother had described his father, he knew his body would probably develop like his. To be so young, he was impressed with the ripples in his midsection, the width of his back, and the bulk on his arms, as was everyone else who had noticed the transformation he'd made during his stay at the Richmond group home.

Both the staff and the other kids had watched in amazement as Treacherous engaged in strenuous workouts, consisting of pull-ups, pushups, and dips throughout the day. He was the biggest kid in the group home.

Standing at five foot nine and weighing in at a solid 185 pounds, for the most part, Treacherous's appearance was enough for the other kids to keep their distance. That was the way he liked it. He had no friends at the group home and he didn't want any. Everyone, including the staff, treated him as if he was from another planet. No one really said anything to him, and his interactions with them were the same.

By the time Treacherous had completed his ten sets, showered, groomed, and dressed, the Virginia sun was just peeking through the window of the room, letting him know it was time for breakfast. All the other kids were just climbing out of their beds and heading to the bathroom. Treacherous could feel a set of eyes on him as he tied his shoelace. When he looked up, his suspicion was confirmed. One of his roommates was delivering a cold stare in his direction as he stood waiting in line for the bathroom. It was the same stare Treacherous had caught the kid shooting at him on three other occasions. The kid's name was Eric Allen, and he had only been at the group home for two and a half months. Eric had been ordered by the court to remain at the group home until he turned eighteen, according to what Treacherous had overheard.

Eric was a chubby, fair-skinned sixteen-year-old, a few inches shorter than Treacherous, with a big afro you could often find him patting as he talked. He often shared his street tales with the six other kids who occupied the attic when it was time to return to their room for the evening. Treacherous never entertained Eric's stories. All he talked about were the hustles he had supposedly indulged in. Apparently, he had done everything from selling drugs to holding up convenient stores and robbing people. He bragged about how he had gotten away with an abundance of riches and merchandise. None of the stories interested Treacherous, though, especially since none could compare to the ones he continuously read in his mother's journals.

The only thing that stood out during Eric's stories was the fact that they mostly took place in the Seven Cities, where Treacherous's family was from. Through Eric's stories, Treacherous learned that he was from the Tidewater Park Projects in Norfolk, which were the same housing projects Treacherous's father and grandfather were from. While Eric had the other kids in awe with his tales, Treacherous sought entertainment in the real-life stories of his parents. Although the two had never said a word to one another, it was evident that Eric didn't like Treacherous, so it did not come as a surprise to him that the person staring at him was, in fact, Eric Allen.

Treacherous met Eric's stare with an even colder one. The two remained locked until one of the kids tapped Eric on the shoulder and informed him that it was his turn to use the bathroom. Before he disappeared into the bathroom, Eric cracked the knuckles of his balled-up fist. Treacherous shook his head and continued tying his sneakers.

Treacherous sat in the corner as he always did with his plate on his lap while the others sat and ate their breakfast at the tables. When he had first arrived, the staff allowed him to sit off in his eating spot out of sympathy for his situation, but, later, when they tried to get him to join the others, he outright refused. Eventually, they got tired of Treacherous's refusals and gave up.

Treacherous slowly ate his eggs and toast. Then, he chased it with a carton of milk as he watched Eric, who was also watching him out the corner of his eye. Although he did not fear anything or anyone, something about Eric had Treacherous feeling uneasy. He could not figure out why, out of all mornings, the kid Eric had decided to have a problem with him. Treacherous stood up and made his way over to the trash can to discard the empty Styrofoam tray and empty milk container. Rather than play the staring game with Eric for the second time that morning, he decided to look straight ahead and pretend Eric didn't even exist. As he neared him, Treacherous detected movement from Eric's direction and instinctively stepped to the side.

"Watch where you're goin', you retarded muthafucka," Eric chimed as he pulled his size-twelve shoe back in after a failed attempt to trip Treacherous. Treacherous made no reaction. He maintained his composure and continued to walk to the garbage can. His back was met with an array of snickers and giggles from Eric's entourage. That was the first time Treacherous had actually felt embarrassed, and he didn't know why. Usually, the other kids showed him respect or simply stayed out of his way. His resentment toward Eric intensified for making him the butt of the joke. Treacherous wondered what his dad or even his mother, for that matter, would have done in a situation like the one he had just endured. He excused the answers that had instantly popped in his head and made a beeline to the back door of the group home, headed to the recreation area.

Treacherous took a deep breath, knowing he had to pass the table again where Eric and his crew of jackals sat. Just as he was within ear range, the words that spilled out of Eric's mouth tore into Treacherous like hot slugs:

"That's why his mother tried to kill him 'cause he's a fuckin'—"

Eric never got to finish his sentence. His words were interrupted and drowned out by the first puncture to his pudgy neck with the ballpoint pen Treacherous plunged into it.

"Fuck you! Fuck you!" Treacherous bellowed as he repeatedly stabbed Eric with the ink pen he had used to mark down his workout sets. Blood sprayed all over the faces of those who, just seconds ago, had participated in laughing at him. Their laughs had now turned into cries. With all of his might, Treacherous hammered the pen in and out of his victim's neck. Those closest to the attack could hear the suction cup sound the ink pen made as it entered and exited. Eric went in and out of consciousness as Treacherous overpowered him. It took every staff member in the house, which consisted of four women and two men, to pry Treacherous away from Eric. Blood continued to spray everywhere as young Eric lay there, slumped over on the table and fighting for his life.

"Somebody! Get a towel!" one of the women who were trying to restrain Treacherous yelled in the direction of the other kids. Despite the adults holding on to him, Treacherous did not put up a fight. Instead, he stood there and stared at Eric, who stared back at him like he had done earlier that morning. Only this time, Eric's eyes were wide-eyed and lifeless. All Treacherous could think about was what Eric had said that had pushed him to attack.

After receiving towels and other first aid equipment, the female staffers released Treacherous and left the men to restrain him. All the other kids stood in horror. None of them dared to look at Treacherous out of fear of being his next victim.

Moments later, sirens could be heard wailing in the air. The sirens were enough to break the trance Treacherous had fallen into. There was no doubt in his mind that they were coming for him. Treacherous knew he didn't have much time.

"Get off me!" he yelled as he tried to get away, but the male staffers only tightened their grip.

"Calm down, Treach," one of them ordered as their grip became even firmer.

"I said get the fuck off of me!" Treacherous roared before breaking free of one of the staff members and throwing him off balance.

The other staff member immediately sprang into action. None of the staff had considered the inner strength one possessed when fueled by anger, and that was what Treacherous had in his favor. The male staffer's intentions failed when Treacherous crouched down and delivered a right hook with all of his being into his groin area. He crouched over instantly.

Treacherous wasted no time taking flight. He bolted up the steps that led to his room. Without hesitation, he reached under his mattress and snatched up his mother's journals. His adrenaline was now in overdrive, and his mind was moving at a rapid pace. He could hear the walkie-talkies down below and everyone snitching him out, revealing his whereabouts. One of the things he had learned from reading his mother's memoirs was that his parents never gave up without a fight. Their motto had always been "No retreat; no surrender," and now it was his.

Treacherous rushed over to the bedroom window. Then, he climbed out and onto the roof. He took one look over the roof and saw that the jump was at least fifteen feet, but he was going to rely on the bushes to break his fall. Without giving it a second thought, Treacherous exhaled and jumped off the roof.

As planned, he landed in the bushes. Despite the bushes easing the fall, they did not serve as the type of cushion Treacherous had hoped for. The fall had nearly knocked the wind out of him, and it dazed him for a few seconds, but, once he had regained his bearings, he gathered up the journals and slowly lifted himself up. Just as he was about to take flight for a second time, total darkness overcame him.

Chapter 3

Treacherous awoke to a chill. The blower from the ceiling blanketed him with cold air. His body was sore, and he had a splitting headache. Both the T-shirt and sweatpants he wore were torn. He knew his ripped clothing and soreness could be credited to his jumping off the roof and into the bushes. The handcuffs that attached his left wrist to the metal railing on the wall were enough confirmation of where he was, but he had no clue how he had gotten there. He was relieved to see his mother's journals lying next to him on the wooden bench. With his free hand, he pulled the journals closer to him. Then, he reached for the spot that was throbbing in the back of his head. He winced from the pain that his touch had caused. He could feel a knot on the back of his head along with dried blood. As he felt around to see if he had any more head injuries, his examination was interrupted.

"Yeah, you little fuck. I bet that'll teach you not to run from the police," the red-faced, overweight officer stated proudly.

Treacherous remained silent.

"Yeah, you little niggers are all the same. All hardcore when you're out there killing each other and selling your dope, but y'all turn into little pussies when you get caught."

The officer grabbed his belt buckle and hiked up his uniform pants as if they were falling down. Treacherous massaged the outer part of his head injury in an attempt to ease the pain while the officer carried on.

"You're lucky I didn't knock your goddamn head off your shoulders, you little prick!"

The officer leaned into the bars and made an attempt to reach for Treacherous, who leaned away.

"There ain't no ink pens in here, you sick little fuck!" the officer said, antagonizing Treacherous. "You're going to fry," he added.

"Rufus, that's enough," a commanding voice said out of nowhere.

Treacherous noticed the sarcastic grin that flashed across Officer Rufus's face as he said, "Yes, sir, Captain." He turned around and saluted. Right before he moved away from the cell, he turned and faced Treacherous.

"I'll see you later, dipshit," he whispered. Then, he made his exit.

As Officer Rufus exited, the face behind the voice that had instructed him to cease his verbal attack on Treacherous appeared. To Treacherous's surprise, the voice belonged to a black man. He noticed the man held a manila folder in his hand.

"Are you okay, kid?" the captain asked.

Treacherous continued to remain silent. Another thing he had learned from reading about his parents was to never trust the police, no matter the color of their skin. Having witnessed the death of his mother at the hands of a black policeman was also more than enough for him to distrust and dislike any type of law enforcement.

"My name is Captain James Stanton. I'm with the Richmond County PD. I'm going to need to ask you some questions." Captain Stanton walked over to the wall and retrieved the chair that was posted up against it. He pulled it over to the cell and took a seat.

"Can you tell me what happened between you and Mr. Allen?" Captain Stanton asked.

Treacherous stared at him oddly, as if he had just asked a confusing question, but that was not the case. He revisited the incident in his mind, trying to figure out what had happened.

"I need you to tell me why you attacked Mr. Allen," the captain said, rephrasing his question.

Still, Treacherous said nothing. Instead, he sat in a daze as the images of Eric sped through his mind. His thoughts went back to the staring game he and Eric had played early that morning, and to the snickering of the other kids. His thoughts switched to the comment that sent him off the deep end, and to the countless stabs he had delivered to Eric's neck.

The captain scratched his head in frustration and exhaled. Then, he offered, "Look, kid. I'm sure you didn't mean for things to happen the way they turned out. You're just a kid, but I can't help you if you don't help me understand what happened back there at that group home."

If Treacherous had heard anything the captain said, he gave no indication. His blank stare only heightened the captain's frustration. "You see this?" The captain pulled out a photo of Eric Allen's deceased body. "This is what's going to have you in a place like this for the rest of your life unless you tell me something and make me understand!" The captain's frustration could be heard in his voice.

Treacherous glanced at the picture of Eric. He noticed that Eric's eyes were now closed and that his body looked bluish as he lay in the nude. The only thing Treacherous could think about was how Eric wouldn't be staring at him, or anyone else for that matter, anymore. The thought caused him to smile on the inside, or so he thought. Apparently, the smile had managed to surface on the outside.

"You think this is funny, kid?" The captain moved closer to the bars and asked, "You think taking a life is a joke?"

He slipped Eric's picture back inside the envelope. Then, he pulled out two more.

"Are these funny to you?" the captain bellowed, flashing the two photos at Treacherous.

Treacherous stared at the photos long and hard. It took a minute for him to figure out who the male and female were in the two pictures. Like Eric, their bodies were also blue and their eyes were closed. When the realization of the identities kicked in, Treacherous turned away from them.

"Not so funny anymore, huh?" the captain spat. He hated having to resort to such measures, but he needed answers. "Now, unless you want to spend the rest of your life in prison, you need to help me understand why you attacked and killed Eric Allen."

Treacherous replied by turning his back to Captain Stanton. As far as he was concerned, he didn't have anything to say to the captain.

Captain Stanton shook his head in disbelief. His patience had officially run out with Treacherous. "Suit yourself, kid."

Then, he stood up and said, "Hopefully, you'll remember that I tried to help you before you end up like your parents."

The captain was so caught up in shaking his head out of frustration that he never even noticed Treacherous's sudden movement. He felt the liquid penetrate his left eye as he heard Treacherous's baritone voice yell, "Fuck you!"

Once again, Treacherous flew into a blind rage at the mention of his parents. Luckily for the captain, the glob of spit Treacherous delivered to his face caused him to move out of reaching distance of him. With his free hand,

Treacherous had tried to grab hold of the captain, but he fell short.

"Fuck you! Fuck you!" he chanted as he had before when he attacked Eric Allen.

The captain stood back and watched as Treacherous ranted and raved. He no longer saw the young kid he had seen moments ago when he first entered the booking area. He had been in law enforcement long enough to recognize what the symptoms of Treacherous's actions meant. He saw the murderous glare in Treacherous's eyes. He knew there was nothing he could do or say to calm Treacherous. All he could do was leave him be. He knew the matter was deeper and was more than even he could handle. With that being his thought, the captain made his exit.

"Don't worry, kid. We're going to get you some help," the captain said right before closing the door behind him.

Chapter 4

Treacherous sat in the chair with his hands folded. He scanned the enormous room. As he conducted his evaluation, what stood out the most were the various plaques and awards hanging on the walls of the office. In front of him sat a gold-plated sign that read GREGORY FLANNIGAN, PH.D.

"Hello, Treacherous. My name is Dr. Flannigan. How are you feeling this morning?"

Treacherous noticed a manila envelope sitting on the doctor's desk. His mother's memoirs, also, lay on the desk alongside the folder. He had no clue why he was in a doctor's office, let alone why they had transferred him from the Richmond County Jail to a medical facility and not a juvenile detention center.

On the previous evening, as they arrived, Treacherous peered out the side of the police car window and noticed the sign in front of the institution. He was not familiar with the first word on the sign, so he could not pronounce it in his head or determine its meaning. It wasn't until he was escorted to the front of the large house and met at the door by two men—one Hispanic, the other black, and both dressed in all-blue uniforms—that he realized he was at a hospital and not a juvenile facility.

He watched as one of the officers thumbed through some papers on a clipboard that had been handed to him by one of the orderlies. After flipping through the pages, the officer signed the last page. He also handed one of the men a manila envelope. Treacherous was sure it was his mother's journals. He found it strange when one of the officers released the handcuffs from his wrists. Then, the officer and his partner made their way back to the car, leaving Treacherous standing there with the two orderlies. The only thing that he could conjure up was that he was being given another chance and was being placed into a securer group home, which may have been a part of the hospital. That was his theory as to why the place had favored a house, he had thought at the time.

He looked around as he followed the two men farther into the ward. Kids in his age group were sprinkled throughout the room. All eyes were on him as he glided through the hallway, matching the two men's strides. *Why are they all looking at me so strange? Is something wrong? Do I have something on my face?* Treacherous wondered. They actually looked odd to him. Although he felt fine, they made him feel self-conscious. He looked down at himself and did a quick body scan while wiping his face. He realized he was good.

As they got to the end of the hall, Treacherous couldn't help but notice a girl off in the corner. Her skin was the color of caramel. She was alone and staring out of a huge window.

"Hi, I'm Sally. What's your name?"

His attention was diverted by a young white girl who had appeared out of nowhere and was now standing in front of him. Treacherous stared at her oddly as she stood just inches away from his face, waving and smiling. He noticed that she still had her baby teeth and they appeared to be razor sharp, like that of a vampire's. Her skin was even pale like one, noticed Treacherous. Her hair was dirty blond and she wore it in pigtails.

"Sally, go sit down," one of the men instructed as they led Treacherous to an open window where a heavyset black lady sat. She wore a nurse's hat on top of her jet-black hair pulled back in a bun and was dressed all in white. Treacherous instantly caught the disgusted look the lady shot at him when she looked up. Her name tag read ARETHA JOHNSON. She rolled her eyes at Treacherous as she stood up. She instructed the two orderlies to follow her. Treacherous noticed how her shoes made a funny noise while her wide hips swayed from left to right as she walked. She came to a complete stop once she reached the metal door that had 2A written on it.

"This will be your room," she spat at Treacherous. "The doctor will see you in the morning," she added once Treacherous was inside.

Then, she exited the room and slammed the door behind her. Treacherous lay back on the bed. It was barely big enough for an average-size kid, let alone someone his size. He tossed his hands behind his head and gazed up at the ceiling. Images of his mother and father appeared. They looked down lovingly at him. He smiled at their sudden presence. Then, he heard his mother's voice say, "You gotta trust Mommy on this, okay, baby?"

Those were the last words he'd heard before drifting off.

"Were you able to get any rest?" Treacherous heard Dr. Flannigan ask, bringing him completely back to the present.

Treacherous pretended not to hear the question. He just sat there and stared out the window behind the doctor. His actions caused the doctor to turn and look out the window too.

"It's going to be a beautiful day in Richmond today." Dr. Flannigan smiled. "Don't you think?"

His question received no response.

"Treacherous, I understand you're afraid and—"

"I'm not scared of nothing," Treacherous lashed out, before Dr. Flannigan could finish his sentence, catching him by surprise.

"I apologize," the doctor offered. "Yes, you seem to be a brave young man, especially after all that you've gone through over the past couple of years," he agreed, trying a different approach. He scanned Treacherous's file.

Treacherous made no indication that he agreed with the doctor. Although he had previously read the majority of what the file contained, Dr. Flannigan reviewed the information pertaining to Treacherous and his parents. He shook his head as he skimmed through the news clipping with the headline BONNIE & CLYDE OF THE NEW MILLENNIUM. He remembered watching the standoff between Treacherous's father and the authorities over fifteen years ago on the news and wondered what had driven the couple to such lengths. As he came to the next clipping about Treacherous's mother, he was filled with sympathy as he viewed the photo under the headline that read ARMORED CAR ROBBER GANGSTER MOM THREATENS TO KILL SON. As a psychiatrist, the picture of Treacherous's mother holding a gun to her son's head spoke volumes to the doctor. He was sure the psyches of both of young Treacherous's parents were unbalanced and abnormal and wondered how much had been passed on genetically. He had read the summary of what had taken place between Treacherous and the deceased kid at the group home, but the photos told another story, and that was the story the doctor was interested in.

"Treacherous, I'd like to ask you some questions," the doctor said. "Now, these are not trick questions or questions to try to hurt you or offend you. If you don't like the question, then you don't have to answer it, and I'll move on to the next one. Fair enough?"

There was a brief pause.

"I guess you didn't like my first question." The doctor smiled for the second time. Again, he was met with silence.

"Treacherous, do you know why you are here?" Dr. Flannigan asked.

Treacherous stared at him as if he was speaking a foreign language. The fact of the matter was that Treacherous had no idea why he was at the hospital. Still, he didn't answer the doctor.

Dr. Flannigan sensed that Treacherous was pondering something. "Treacherous, a judge ordered you here and requested a psychological evaluation be done on you. The only way I can do that and help you, too, is if you let me. I understand all of this may be quite confusing to you, but, if you just answer a few questions, things may become a little clearer for the both of us. Then, we can figure out how to make things better," Dr. Flannigan suggested empathetically.

Treacherous studied the doctor as he spoke. The words "make things better" resonated in Treacherous's young mind. He was still trying to process what had happened back at the group home and why. It was all a blur to him. He wanted to answer the doctor, but, for some reason, he just couldn't bring himself to do it. Instead, he responded with a shake of his head.

"I don't understand," Dr. Flannigan said, realizing he had just made a breakthrough. "Are you saying no, you're not going to answer the questions, or, no, you don't know why you're here?"

Treacherous rolled his eyes in frustration. "Why am I here?" he answered with a question.

Now, the doctor felt he was getting somewhere. "You're here because you hurt someone, Treacherous, and you hurt him really bad, and nobody but you knows why. We're trying to see if you meant to or not." Dr. Flannigan leaned forward with his hands clasped and continued, "And it is my job to find out with your help, of course, so you never hurt anyone else again. So, can you tell me why you attacked the young man back at the group home?"

Treacherous listened as the doctor spoke. His question caused Treacherous's mind to roam. Images of Eric played in his mind. He could hear the words that had triggered him. They had echoed in his head right before he launched his attack. Then, he saw the final scene with him on top of Eric, plunging the ink pen into his neck repeatedly. He watched in awe. He could not believe that he and the person he was watching were one and the same. It was as if he were having an out-of-body experience. He witnessed Eric's blood spray his deranged-looking face. From there, everything seemed to move at warp speed. Then, all of a sudden, Treacherous's mind went pitch black. The doctor's voice brought him back to the present as he regained his vision. Treacherous noticed the doctor was holding up a photo.

"So, tell me what made you so angry that it caused you to react in this manner."

The photo was the same one of Eric the chief had shown him back at the holding cell. Treacherous looked at the doctor and shrugged his shoulders. Then, he shifted his eyes to his lap.

"Of course you know," Dr. Flannigan offered. "Just take your time and think. What did he say or do to you to upset you so much?"

Again, Treacherous responded with a shrug of the shoulders. He could feel his armpits beginning to perspire and little beads of sweat forming on his forehead despite the air condition doing a good job of keeping the office at a cool temperature.

"Did he call you any names or threaten to do anything to you?" Dr. Flannigan continued.

Treacherous shook his head just enough for Dr. Flannigan to see. Dr. Flannigan let out a light sigh.

"There had to be something, Treacherous." He leaned forward with his fingers intertwined. "I'm having a difficult time believing that a young man as bright and humble as you would just attack someone for no reason at all," Dr. Flannigan stated compassionately.

Treacherous raised his head and stared the doctor square in his eyes. He could not bring himself to trust the doctor.

Dr. Flannigan met his stare. After a few long seconds, he leaned back and gathered up Treacherous's file. As far as he was concerned, that day's session was over. Although he had broken ground, in his mind, he had really gotten nowhere. Just as he was about to close Treacherous's file, he noticed out of his peripheral vision that Treacherous was watching him. When he looked up, Treacherous quickly lowered his gaze, but not before Dr. Flannigan could catch what he had been staring at. At that moment, a bright light lit up, and it, suddenly, all made sense to the doctor.

"I'll tell you what I think," Dr. Flannigan stated. When Treacherous raised his head to look at him, he continued, "I think that young man Eric said something that hurt your feelings so bad and made you so angry that you didn't know how to control your feelings and emotions, so you just reacted."

Dr. Flannigan studied Treacherous's body language. He knew the statement had gotten Treacherous's attention.

"I, also, believe that you were not aware, at the time, that you were hurting Eric the way you were or that you meant to take his life. I believe you only lashed out against him to make him stop saying whatever hurtful things he had said or was saying to you. And since you seem to be a very strong young man, I really don't think he could have said anything about you that could have hurt your feelings or upset you. But . . ." Dr. Flannigan let his word linger. "I do believe that it would hurt or upset you if he said something about someone you loved or cared about, especially if that person or people are no longer here."

Judging by the slight change on Treacherous's face, Dr. Flannigan knew he had scratched more than just the surface. Treacherous did his best to remain stone-faced, but he knew his eyes had confirmed the doctor's theory.

"Treacherous, did Eric say something bad about your parents?" Dr. Flannigan asked, patting the folder lying on his desk. "I need to know if you want me to help you."

Treacherous's eyes glanced at the folder in front of the doctor once again. Then, he looked back at the doctor.

"Treacherous, tell me!" Dr. Flannigan insisted. "Did you attack Eric Allen because he said something about your parents?"

Treacherous's breathing increased, and his chest swelled with each breath. His head throbbed as a sharp pain jolted the side of his left temple. Dr. Flannigan noticed the transition and slipped his hand underneath his desk.

"Treacherous, try to calm yourself. It's okay. I'm not here to hurt you. I'm only here to help you. I just need you to answer the question. What did Eric say about your—"

"Mind your fuckin' business, mu'fucka!" The words boomed out of Treacherous's mouth like a bullet from a .44 Magnum as he shot up out of his chair.

Fear displayed itself all over Dr. Flannigan's Hershey-toned face. "Treacherous, please!" he pleaded, but his words fell on deaf ears.

Treacherous had transformed into a blind rage. He was now foaming at the mouth like a rabid dog. "You don't know shit about me or my family!" he bellowed.

Tears now streamed down his face. He grabbed hold of the closest object within reach. Dr. Flannigan pushed back from his desk and stood horrified on the opposite side. He backpedaled away from his desk until he felt his back hit the wall.

"If you ask me anything else about my family, I'll fuckin'—"

The dosage of the drug in the needle the nurse injected into Treacherous had an immediate effect on him. Within seconds he was sedated. His body crashed to the floor, making a loud thud. He was in such a rage that he never heard the nurse and orderlies enter the office. The puny doctor was thankful for the silent alarm that had been placed under his desk for situations such as this. That was the first time he'd had to use it since it had been installed ten years ago.

"Are you all right, sir?" Orderly Ron asked.

"Yes, I'm fine. Please just take him to his room." Dr. Flannigan waved them off as he gathered up Treacherous's file and manila folder. "And make sure you strap him down for the night. I don't want any more incidents," he added as he opened the file cabinet and placed the file and manila envelope inside another folder that contained Treacherous's name.

"Yes, sir," Orderly Joe said, nodding.

"The dose I gave him will last through the evening," Nurse Johnson assured the doctor.

Treacherous could hear the sounds of voices but could not move. He lay helpless on the floor, staring up at the ceiling. He could feel numerous hands grabbing hold of him and could feel his body being lifted into the air. Treacherous's vision was somewhat blurry from the injection. As the orderlies carried him out of the doctor's office, an image of his mother appeared on the ceiling. Their eyes met, and, for that brief moment, that was all that had mattered to him. He saw the half smile appear across his mother's face. He noticed her lips were moving, but he could not make out the words nor could he hear them, but that did not matter, because, in his mind, he had already imagined what she was saying to him. Treacherous returned her smile. Then, he closed his eyes. As he drifted off, he knew there was nothing to be worried about; his mother had confirmed that everything was going to be okay.

Chapter 5

A month and a half later

"Treacherous! Time to get up. Today's your lucky day," the orderly announced.

The sound of the door to his room being unlocked had already caused his eyes to shoot open, rendering him wide awake.

"Doc says you can come out to the dayroom."

It had been nearly six weeks since the incident in Dr. Flannigan's office. For the first ten days, Treacherous had been strapped to his bed and intravenously fed a high dosage of Thorazine twice a day to ease his aggression. Once he had been released from the restraints, they served him the drug in liquid form. Treacherous did not know what was happening to him, but he knew the drug was the cause of it. The drug made him sluggish and somewhat unbalanced. He often found himself zoning out and drooling.

Initially, he would just sit and stare whenever the doctor came for their early morning sessions. He knew the longer he rebelled and resisted the doctor's treatment, the longer he would remain in the state he was in. After awhile, he simply gave in and responded to Dr. Flannigan's questions with a nod or shake of the head. As a reward, Dr. Flannigan changed his medication dosage. It was not his intent to have Treacherous become dependent on the drug or to cause an imbalance, so he reduced the dosage gradually until, finally, he was switched to a milder medication with fewer side effects.

A few weeks prior, the doctor had informed Treacherous that the judge had mandated him to undergo treatment and be remanded to the mental hospital, based on the evaluation he had submitted. Treacherous was told that another evaluation would be submitted to the courts when he reached the age of eighteen. Hearing that he had to be at the facility for almost another three years caused Treacherous to become a little depressed. He knew the only way he was going to make it out of the institution was by doing what he needed to do to convince the doctor and the judge that he should be released, and that became his plan.

Treacherous rolled over and peered at the orderly. He thought his ears had deceived him.

"I'm serious, man. I just got the green light to let you come out," Orderly Ron beamed. "It'll do you some good," he added. "Between me and you," he said, lowering his voice, "I never agreed with them keeping you locked in here like this in the first place. This ain't no way to treat a kid, regardless of what you did. It's inhumane."

Treacherous knew that Orderly Ron meant every word he had just spoken. Treacherous didn't like any of the other staff members, but he half-assed liked Ron. From day one, Ron had been nice to him, while the others treated him like he was an animal or a retard. It was Orderly Ron who had actually increased his knowledge about motorcycles, thanks to the magazines he often brought in for him to read after he had bounced back to his normal self. Treacherous had longed for the day to be let out of the room and allowed to roam around in a much bigger space, and the day had finally come. The small five-by-eight room made him feel like a caged dog.

Treacherous flung the covers off of himself. He stood and stretched. Then, he kneeled beside his bed. Orderly Ron was used to seeing Treacherous perform his early morning ritual. He backed out of Treacherous's room and let him be.

Chapter 6

"Baby, please take your medicine," Nurse Johnson requested. Exhaustion was written on her face as she said, "I'm sleepy and not in the mood tonight, and you know I don't want to have to call Ron and Joe and have them take you down." She held a small paper cup that contained one yellow pill and one blue pill in her left hand and a small bottle of water under the same arm.

Baby stood with her right foot and left shoulder leaning against the wall of her room. She had a crazed look on her face.

"Are you serious, Baby? Okay. Suit yourself!" Nurse Johnson said as she backed out of the room. She closed and locked the door behind her. Baby gave her the finger as she exited the room. When the door shut, she took a deep breath and prepared herself for what was to come next.

It only took five minutes before Baby heard the key sliding into the lock. The two orderlies stepped into the room. Nurse Johnson followed them.

Without wasting any time, Joe smiled at Baby. Then, he charged at her. He made a failed attempt to grab Baby by the waist, but Baby sidestepped him and delivered a powerful blow to his temple, causing him to buckle slightly. While Orderly Joe was trying to keep from hitting the floor, Orderly Ron tried to slip behind Baby to subdue her. Baby quickly spun around and locked horns with the orderly who was nearly twice her size.

"Calm down!" Orderly Ron spat as he tussled with Baby. Baby could feel him overpowering her with his strength. She dropped her head into his chest and opened her mouth wide. Orderly Ron screamed in agony as Baby bit through his uniform and into his flesh. The pain was enough to make him release his hold on her. Nurse Johnson stood frozen in horror at the sight. There was no doubt in her mind that she was no match for Baby, which was why she stood clear of the battle between Baby and the orderlies.

Baby tried to finish Orderly Ron off by swinging a wild right hook. She just missed him but connected with the chin of Orderly Joe, who was trying to grab hold of her too, since he had regained his composure.

"Shit! You bitch," Joe spat.

Baby was still swinging her arms and kicking her feet in an attempt to fight them both. At fifteen years old, 120 pounds, and with a great deal of inner strength, she had done a superb job against two grown men, but she was bought to a halt by a migraine headache that appeared out of nowhere. That was the break the orderlies needed. The excruciating pain caused Baby to drop to her knees. In a matter of seconds, the two men were able to get a firm hold of Baby.

Orderly Joe roughly snatched her up and threw her on to the bed like a rag doll. Her body bounced on the thin mattress. Her head just missed the iron rail that served as a headboard. Baby was still kicking and screaming, trying to land a blow anywhere that could possibly hurt, while trying to fight off the throbbing pain inside her head. The only thing that finally stopped both Baby and the pain was when Orderly Joe used his body weight to pin her down. Nurse Johnson ran over and stuck her in her left arm with a needle the size of a pencil. The injection served its purpose. Baby became numb as the liquid flowed through her veins. It felt like heat on the back of her neck as it moved straight to her brain, halting her movements.

The medication made Baby drowsy. She went in and out of consciousness. Baby gazed at her caretakers as they filed out of the small space. She closed her eyes. She could hear the door being closed and locked.

Once she heard the final click, she slowly opened her eyes and saw Orderly Joe staring at her through the small block of glass. The sight of him made the pit of Baby's stomach boil. She closed her eyes tightly to block the image of the monster at the glass.

That was fun! Baby thought as a tear formed in the corner of her right eye. She turned her face to the wall. As the teardrop slowly slid down the side of her face, images of her parents' faces, standing in a courtroom, appeared.

Baby had been committed to a mental institution until she turned eighteen, after a judge deemed her temporarily insane. As the thought of her parents replaced the pain that she felt from the fight, more tears surfaced. Not because of the hurt she knew she had caused them but because she wasn't sure why they were hurt. Baby didn't know if it was because she had been convicted, the fact she had been labeled insane, or the embarrassment she was supposed to have caused them. They were clear that what she had done was a reflection of them somehow. At least, her mother had made that very clear. According to her mother, she had brought humiliation to her father, who was a decorated police officer, and shame to her, being viewed as an ideal wife, exceptional mother, and a pillar of the community. Baby's mother's tears brought on a sense of confusion as the judge sentenced her to the mental institution. In her heart, she hoped that her mother was crying for her, but she knew that that was probably not the case. Her father just mumbled for the most part, claiming that he didn't understand where he had gone wrong. The words "My family was supposed to be damn near perfect" were the knives that pierced Baby's heart ever since her father had spoken them.

Even as she lay on a thin wool blanket with springs sticking her in the back, Baby wasn't sure how her nightmare had started. Her world had been almost perfect. She was an only child who had wanted for nothing. Her father had given her everything she wanted, and, even though her mother hated that she got whatever she wanted, she had spoiled her too.

Slowly, exhaustion set in. Baby's eyes grew weak. Then, the dreams followed. Sleep slipped past the wall Baby had tried so fiercely to hold up. Not even the drugs could have stopped them as she drifted off.

"Stay still and relax," were the opening words that had haunted Baby in her dreams repeatedly over the last five years.

"That hurts," Baby said. Her voice was tiny and confused.

"Come on now. Just stay still," the voice whispered. "Just let me see."

Some nights, the dream would go further. At times, Baby felt as if she was unable to wake herself from them. Sometimes, she would wake up screaming and sweating profusely. As bad as she wanted someone to come to her rescue, she knew that no one ever would. When they had first started, she thought it was going to drive her crazy. Then, she realized how to stop the nightmares or, at least, slow them down.

Chapter 7

From afar, Baby could hear the morning bell and the doors opening along the hall.

"Time to get up," Orderly Joe stated, opening Baby's room door.

Five minutes later, Orderly Joe entered Baby's room. Joe was a big Spanish man who stood around six two or maybe taller. What stood out about him was that his arms appeared to be way too big for his body, and he always smelled of stale cigarettes. Baby never liked being around Joe for too long. He made her feel that familiar feeling that Baby was constantly running from, and it made her skin crawl.

"Get your stuff. You know the routine by now," Joe said.

Nurse Johnson came in behind him and asked, "How are you feeling this morning?"

Baby, barely awake, slid her legs off the bunk and placed her feet on the floor while using both of her hands to brace herself as she attempted to stand. She searched the room for her flip-flops, as they had been tossed around during the fight. One was in the far corner of the room under the writing table while the other had landed under the bed. As Baby bent down to get the flip-flop, she felt lightheaded. She didn't want Nurse Johnson to notice, so she stayed down until her head cleared.

"Let's go! I don't have all day to play with your ass," Joe said, still upset behind the injuries from the previous night.

"Can you stand?" Nurse Johnson asked.

Without answering, Baby stood to her feet.

"Well, I guess so. So, here are your meds. Let's take them without a problem today, okay?"

Baby and Nurse Johnson had been playing the same game almost every day since Baby arrived at her unit. On the first day, while she was attempting to give Baby her meds, she made the mistake of taking her eyes off the newbie for just a second, and, before she knew it, Nurse Johnson found herself stumbling backward from a punch to the eye. The hit from the tiny teenager dazed her just long enough to allow Baby to get in a kick to the knee and an open hand smack to the face. All of this was done before the orderly was able to get into the room. Baby, then, grabbed her by her ponytail and flung her to the bed before she was finally subdued by the orderlies.

This day was no different than the others. Baby felt a little weak from the shot and some minor pain around her ankles and across her thigh.

"I brought you some new toiletries," Nurse Johnson said pleasantly as if nothing had ever happened the previous night. She waited for a response from Baby, but, as always, there was nothing.

Baby glanced at the package that the nurse had brought and nodded her head. That was the most communication that could be expected from Baby, outside of the violent behavior that seemed to come whenever the thought crossed her mind.

As Baby started the walk from her room to the shower, she thought she was going to be sick as she dragged herself down the musty hall. Her feet felt heavy. She felt as if she was lugging them along instead of them assisting her in her movements.

Each morning, Baby's routine was the same. She took the same walk to the showers. Each morning she would notice the freckle-faced girl with the deep red hair. Today was different. The redheaded girl who had always greeted Baby with her smile through the glass block window of her cell door whenever Baby walked by was not there that day. Baby had no idea who the redhead was or why she was in that place, but, each day, as Baby walked past her cell, the redhead would smile at her. The smile was a comforting one. It seemed as if the girl knew Baby from somewhere. Realizing that the redhead was not there created a feeling of sadness in Baby that she did not know she could feel. Baby couldn't remember ever feeling sad at the loss of anyone or anything.

When Baby was eight years old, her father had gotten her a kitten. It was a pretty, white kitten they had named Silly. The reason for the name was that, as a kitten, Silly liked to roll herself down the twelve or so stairs in Baby's house. The first time she did it, Baby and her father thought the kitten had hurt herself, but she got up and attempted to run up the steps to do it again. Silly was too small to climb the steps. Baby and her father had laughed so hard that day just watching the kitten trying to climb the first step only to roll herself back down them. They thought that was so silly that they decided that that would be the kitten's name.

When Baby was eleven, she and Silly, who had flourished into a beautiful cat, were at the top of the stairs. Baby watched with a smile on her face as Silly began her famous roll down the stairs. She had no way of knowing her mother had been hanging pictures and had left a hammer on the edge of the very last step. When Silly rolled to the bottom, all Baby heard was Silly's cat cry, followed by the sound of a sickening crack. By the time Baby made her way to the bottom of the steps, Silly lay there with her green eyes open and blood seeping from the side of her head, staining the beige carpet. The ham-

mer had crushed her skull. Baby's parents, along with both her aunt and uncle, thought she would be heartbroken, but she felt nothing. All she wanted was a new cat.

As Baby entered the recreation room, she scanned the room as she always did, taking note that the redhead was not in the recreation room either. As usual, the room was filled with teenagers. Some were playing games, and some were just walking around as if they were lost.

Baby always went directly to her favorite spot: the bay window at the far end of the recreation room. Baby loved that window. It reminded her of a window that was in her Aunt Jazelle's house. Her aunt's house was located on the outskirts of Richmond. The windows in the front of her house were stained the same way the one bay window in the recreation room was. The only difference was the color. It was stained yellow at the top and had a sky blue design, and her aunt's windows were stained with colorful flowers that created a rainbow in the house when the sun hit them. Baby had spent every summer since she could remember at her Aunt Jazelle's house, riding horses and swimming in the lake or just plain chilling. She had looked forward to it until her aunt had banned her from the house when she was eleven and a half.

At the ward, Baby spent most of her time in the dayroom looking out the yellow and blue stained window, daydreaming about better times. It made her feel calm for a change, even amid all the noise around her. Those stolen moments made the later moments when her head seemed cloudy easier to deal with.

That day, Baby's moment was interrupted by the reflection she saw in the window. Baby could feel and see him watching her as she looked out the window. It wasn't the same feeling she got when Orderly Joe watched her. It was something different, and it made her feel different. She couldn't quite put her finger on it and didn't take much time to figure it out. She knew he didn't realize she could see him in the window. She thought about turning around to let him know, but she decided against it. Instead, she acted as if he wasn't even there.

Baby spent the last thirty minutes daydreaming about what seemed like a past life. The life she had before she became what the newspapers called "a teenage killer." She recalled a time when she was the highlight of her father's day, his pretty baby girl he'd taught to ride a motorcycle and drive a car before she could even touch the pedals of either. She was the honor roll student her mother bragged about to the various committee members, the black belt at the age of eight, and the medal-winning gymnast at age nine. She thought about her life when the walls of her bedroom were painted pink and her pillows and sheets were yellow with pink roses. There was not a stain to be found. Her new life was not of her choosing, and she did not know how to turn back the hands of time, and no one seemed to know how to help.

A tray that fell to the floor to the left of Baby broke her thoughts. When she returned to the real world, Nurse Johnson was standing in front of her.

"It's that time again," Nurse Johnson said, holding a tiny white paper cup and a clear plastic cup.

Baby rolled her eyes.

"Why must you be so difficult?" Nurse Johnson asked frustrated.

Baby responded by sucking her teeth.

"I don't understand how someone with your background can be so messed up in the head. It makes no sense to me, having such good parents and all, and all you want to be is a disappointment!"

Nurse Johnson was so engrossed in chastising Baby that she never saw her rise up from the wall. All in one motion, Baby smacked Nurse Johnson, the cup of pills, and the plastic cup of water. The cup of pills spilled to the floor, while the cold water splashed in Nurse Johnson's face, cooling the sting that Baby's blow had caused.

"You don't know shit, you fat bitch!" Baby cursed before storming off.

As she spun on her heels to head in the direction of the door, she was met by a pair of eyes. A sense of nervousness swept through her body, and she didn't know why. As she walked in his direction, Baby quickly turned her head and looked straight ahead. As she headed for the door, she made sure not to look his way. She could feel his eyes on her with each stride as she got closer to where he sat. She had a feeling that he was going to say something to her once their paths crossed. She knew if she acknowledged his presence, and if he said something to her, she would take her anger and aggression out on him, and she did not want that to be the case. Despite the fact that she had done her best to avoid him, when she walked past, she could still feel his presence. *Why is his vibe so strong?* she wondered as she exited the dayroom.

Chapter 8

Treacherous stood at the top of the dayroom for a moment and took in the scenery. Kids of all ages, sizes, and colors filled the dayroom. Some sat in front of the television watching a rerun of *The Woody Woodpecker Show,* while others walked around or played together or separately with toys provided for them. Treacherous noticed how some of the kids had on regular clothes like him, while some wore hospital gowns. He wondered why.

As he made his way into the dayroom, he noticed the same golden honey-toned girl he had seen when he first arrived, standing by the same window, staring out of it.

Treacherous studied her from afar. Although her tight black tee and denim jeans made her seem tomboyish, from a side profile, Treacherous thought she was pretty. The way she wore her hair gave him a full view of the side of her face. Thoughts of his mother came to mind as he stared at the girl. Her hair was wavy and pulled back in a ponytail, which was the same way he last remembered his mother wearing her hair before she was taken away from him.

He shook the eerie feeling off and found his way over to one of the unoccupied sofa chairs. Treacherous wondered what was wrong with the girl. Judging by the other kids in the facility, he figured she was crazy, retarded, disturbed, or all of the above; but, to him, she looked normal. Treacherous couldn't help but stare in her direction every other minute.

He watched from afar as one of the nurses approached the girl. He could tell by the nurse's body language that something wasn't right. The girl's next move only confirmed Treacherous's assumption. He watched in admiration as she smacked the small paper cup and clear plastic cup out of the nurse's hand and stormed off. Treacherous couldn't help but let out a chuckle as the pills poured out of the paper cup and onto the floor. The water splashed all over the nurse's face. From where he was sitting, it appeared she had also slapped the nurse, but he wasn't sure. Treacherous's eyes followed the girl as she hastily walked in his direction. He was about to say something to her, but, once she had reached the area he sat in, her demeanor made him change his mind. Instead, he watched as she headed out of the recreation room. Moments later, he watched as Orderly Ron and Orderly Joe rushed past him and ran in the girl's direction. For a brief moment, a thought entered his mind to get up and follow them, but, just as quickly as it came, it went.

Chapter 9

The sound of the unlocking metal door caused Baby's eyes to shoot open. Despite being drugged up, she knew she was no longer dreaming. She tried to lift her head but it felt like a ton of bricks.

Suddenly, she could feel hands pulling her legs apart. Baby struggled to snatch her legs away from her attacker, but with no success. Her movements had been hindered by something. The violator's hands slowly moved their way up to her outer thighs. The slowness of the advance created a jolt of heat that ran up Baby's inner thighs. The hands traveled up to her butt cheeks and made their way around to her midsection. Baby felt a tingling sensation, as if she had to use the bathroom. The strange feeling quickly turned into pain as the violators fingers probed and fondled her youthful cave. Baby perspired. Her inner thighs moistened. When she had nightmares, she could normally end them by screaming or falling out of bed, but this was no dream.

"Please," she slurred, fading in and out of consciousness.

She wished it had only been a dream, but she did not have such luck. The injection she had been given since she had been confined to her room hindered her mobility. With what little strength she managed to muster up, she was able to lift her head just enough to see who she knew was touching her. Her heart skipped a beat as it always did as Orderly Joe removed the blanket covering her body and hiked up her hospital gown. He raised her legs. Then, he pulled her panties to one side and buried his head between them.

"Yeah, let me get a taste of this sweetness," he whispered and then planted a kiss on her bottom lips.

Baby squeezed her eyes shut and attempted to ball up her fists. Tears of anger formed underneath her eyelids. She felt herself struggling to move. Her body and mind refused to help her plight. Her vision was blurry, and she was starting to feel a headache coming on.

Orderly Joe ran his hands up and down Baby's body without care or concern. He continued to violate Baby as he inserted two fingers in and out of her. Baby squirmed and mumbled as she tried with all of her might to fight him off. Joe wasn't paying Baby any attention. He stood up, took a step back, and flashed an idiotic smile. He, then, pulled the strings from his scrubs and let them drop to the floor. This would be the first time he had ever had the opportunity to go all the way and he was excited. Baby's eyes grew cold as she clenched her teeth and braced herself.

"You gonna like this, you bitch," Joe whispered into Baby's ear. His breath reeked of stale coffee.

Baby was now breathing hard. She was trying desperately to regain her strength in order to fight Joe off.

"Shit!" Joe cursed.

The sound of the knock on the metal door caused Baby's heart to speed up with confidence. Joe covered Baby's mouth for fear that she might scream. Joe was now faced with a decision. He knew that he had to hurry or risk being caught with his pants down, literally. Joe could feel Baby's heart pounding and could see what he thought to be fear in her eyes. That only added to the blood rushing to his rock hard. Out of all of the young girls he had been molesting and raping since he had been at the institution,

Baby was the only one who had ever had him so turned on. Joe wanted some of her in the worst way. He didn't waste any more time. He pulled Baby's gown up farther, exposing her right breast. He licked his lips at the sight of her B cup. Joe promptly took her nipple in between his teeth, while massaging Baby's clit.

The knock on the door in the distance came again. This time, it was followed by the morning bell.

"Shit! Fuck me!" Joe cursed for a second time.

Joe had no other choice but to get up and make his way out of Baby's room before Nurse Johnson neared.

"You're lucky. But I'm not done with you yet," Joe stated, pulling up his scrubs.

Joe had just finished tying his drawstring when the door flew open. Baby heard Nurse Johnson's squeaky nurse shoes enter the room. She was followed by Orderly Ron. Baby heard them greet Joe. She was fully aware of the fact that Joe was not supposed to be in her room without another orderly or nurse to accompany him. She was sure someone would question his presence, especially with her lying with her body partially exposed, but neither of them said anything.

Instead, Orderly Ron walked back out the room. He gestured for Orderly Joe to follow him while Nurse Johnson pulled Baby's nightgown down over her nudeness and covered her back up with her blanket. She set Baby's meds on the nightstand and turned around. Baby could see Nurse Johnson standing there, shaking her head. Then, she, too, made her way to the door and exited the room. Tears cascaded down Baby's face as the door locked behind Nurse Johnson.

Chapter 10

A month later

Treacherous sat in the corner, looking through one of the motorcycle magazines that Orderly Ron had given him. Out of his peripheral vision, he could see someone enter the dayroom. His attention was immediately drawn to the person when he heard one of the other kids call her name.

A rerun of *Family Matters* could be heard as chatter from the young patients filled the recreation room. He eyed her as she maneuvered through the cluster of bodies that stood in the way of her reaching her preferred spot.

As Baby slid through the remaining teenagers, she noticed he had been watching her. She ignored him and planted herself at the window. As Baby stared past the trees and out into the mountains, once again, she could see the reflection of him in the stained glass. Only this time, the image appeared closer. Baby ignored the figure as she continued to gaze out the window deep in thought.

"Hey."

His voice interrupted her thoughts, but Baby did not reply.

"Pardon me." He spoke again. "Do you mind if I stand here with you?"

He pointed to the spot on the floor right next to Baby. She thought his question was odd as she turned her attention in his direction. Their eyes met for the second time, but, this time, Baby was able to get a good look at him. *There is something inviting about his eyes,* she thought.

He fidgeted with the pages of the magazine as he contemplated his next words, seeing that he had gotten her attention. He said, "My bad, am I interrupting you?"

His voice was low but strong. He watched as Baby shook her head. Her response caused a slight smile to appear across his face. Baby took one step to the left to allow him to step into the window space.

"I see you like this window," Treacherous said, never taking his eyes off the magazine.

Baby just nodded her head, acknowledging his comment.

"Uh, if you don't mind me asking, what's so special about it?"

Baby could hear the nervousness in his voice. She rolled her eyes. She was not one for small talk, but she answered anyway. "It's peaceful," she replied, cutting her eyes over at him.

"Peaceful?" he asked.

"Yeah," she replied. She hoped her tone had expressed her thoughts without hurting his feelings. Surprisingly, he never flinched.

"You know, I seen your work a couple of weeks back."

Baby knew he was referring to the incident that had landed her in her room for thirty days.

"I like how you stood your ground."

If he only knew, she thought.

"You remind me of someone," Treacherous told her.

His statement piqued her curiosity, but she refused to ask him the question. Baby took another good look at him in the window. She studied him, trying her best not to seem obvious. She found him to be attractive. She could tell he was into working out by how well defined his arms were. Baby shook off the thoughts. She didn't know why she was analyzing him the way she was. Although she was slightly attracted to him, his presence was not welcomed. This was her alone time, and he was invading her space.

He stood there with what almost seemed like a grin on his face. He picked up on the fact that she no longer wanted to talk, but he completely ignored it. Instead, he continued.

"You smacked the fuck out of that nurse."

Baby cut her eyes over at him and inhaled. Then, she stared back out the window.

"She was tight as hell. You should have seen her after you walked away. She was barkin' at everybody 'cause they was laughin' and stuff. She was on her knees tryin' to clean up the water, the pills, and all that shit. That was funny."

He smiled at the thought of it, and Baby couldn't resist as the incident resonated in her mind, so she cracked a smile at the thought too. She had been in such a zone that day that she hadn't even thought about what the other people had apparently watched.

"Wow, did I just make you smile?" he asked, after seeing Baby's face light up.

"No," she said, quickly changing her facial expression back to a blank one. It had been a minute since anyone had been able to make her smile like that. She hated that she had allowed him to see it. He noticed how uneasy she was.

"It was good talkin' to you. I didn't mean to bother you. Maybe another time," he said. "By the way, my name is Treacherous."

He extended his hand, and Baby let it linger in the air. She didn't know whether she wanted to shake it.

She hesitated for a moment. Then, while shaking Treacherous's hand, she said, "Baby. My name is Baby."

"Seriously?"

"Yes. You got a problem with that?" She released his hand.

"I didn't mean any disrespect," Treacherous clarified. "What is it short for?"

Baby gave Treacherous a hard sideways look.

Treacherous saw that her demeanor had change.

"Nothing. That's my name," she said sternly.

"I didn't mean to offend you. I just never met anyone with that name before," Treacherous said apologetically.

"You didn't offend me," Baby dryly retorted.

Ever since he had laid eyes on her, Treacherous had thought she resembled his mother physically, but the more she spoke, the more she reminded him of his mother in other ways. *Even down to the unique name,* he thought. His thoughts were invaded by Baby's voice.

"My father gave me that name because he loved me and said I was always going to be his baby."

Treacherous detected some hurt in her voice, but he did not try to pry. "It's a cool name," he replied. "I like it. It's original."

There was an awkward silence for a moment. Baby was the first to break it.

"So, what kinda name is Treacherous? You must be untrustworthy or something," Baby said, turning the tables. She was actually beginning to enjoy having someone to talk to.

Treacherous found no humor in her words, though. "You can trust me," he replied. "And I was named after my father."

"Tsk. Boy, please. I don't even know you," Baby shot back with an attitude.

Treacherous knew she was trying to sound hard, but he ignored it. Ever since the scene with the nurse had taken place, Treacherous wondered if she was as tough as she portrayed herself to be. Treacherous could now see that she was as serious as he had thought, and he was even more impressed.

"How long you gotta be here for?" Treacherous asked.

"You're nosey."

Treacherous smirked and said, "I get out of this fuckin' place when I hit eighteen, hopefully."

In the midst of him talking, someone appeared in between Treacherous and Baby.

"Yo! You done with that magazine, homie?" spat a seventeen-year-old kid named Tony, who stayed in the room across from Treacherous. He was a little bit too aggressive for Treacherous's taste. Treacherous noticed that Baby had caught it as well. That bothered him.

"Yo, dawg! Who you talking to like that?"

The tone in Treacherous's voice quickly switched from the soft-spoken one that had had Baby's ear to one of extreme caution, but Tony didn't back down.

Treacherous could feel his blood beginning to boil. At that moment, he knew he needed to defuse any potential situation rather than spark one.

"I know you see us talking, and, no, I'm not done with it. It's not mine to lend out anyway, so, when I'm done, you can get it from Orderly Ron, a'ight, dawg?" Treacherous answered, giving Tony a stern look.

"Yeah, a'ight." Tony chuckled, looking Baby up and down with lustful eyes. He had been trying to get Baby's attention since she had arrived, but to no avail, and he resented the fact that the new kid was so easily able to. Tony wanted to say more but thought better of it. Although he knew he was older, Treacherous stood three inches over him and outweighed him by at least fifteen pounds. Tony was not sure if he could handle a physical confrontation with him.

"See you later, Baybee," Tony said, letting her name drag.

Baby sucked her teeth.

By then, Treacherous was fuming. He knew Tony was trying to be funny, but he, also, knew how important it was for him to maintain his composure if he wanted to get out of the hospital on time. Treacherous drew it up as being Tony's lucky day but made a mental note of the disrespect. Tony shot Treacherous a rock-hard stare before walking off, whistling.

"You should have smacked fire out that nigga," Baby stated, rolling her eyes in the direction that Tony walked.

"Not worth it," Treacherous replied. His soft-spoken voice had returned.

Baby looked over at Treacherous and rolled her eyes again. She folded her arms and continued to gaze out the window.

"Okay. I'ma leave you alone. It was nice meeting you, though," he said. "Maybe I'll see you here again tomorrow," he quickly added, right before he started his backward walk.

"Maybe," she dryly replied, not bothering to turn around to look at him.

"That's good enough for me."

Unbeknownst to Treacherous, he had left Baby standing at the window with mixed emotions. She had been around plenty of boys before, but none were like Treacherous. He had made her feel some type of way. The boy with the untrustworthy name had sparked an interest in Baby. He had sparked an interest that made her want to explore more.

Chapter 11

"Oh, yeah! Right there. Mmm. Suck that dick," Orderly Joe moaned as he threw his head back and closed his eyes. "I've never had my dick sucked like this before," he confessed.

He looked down and watched as he received the best oral he ever had in his life. The humming and slurping noises she made turned him on. Saliva dripped out of the corners of her mouth as she bobbed up and down on his hardness. He felt like he was on top of the world. It was because of episodes such as this that Orderly Joe loved his job so much. The thought of getting caught while getting his dick sucked or fucking on the job excited him. He was a stone-cold freak and enjoyed the entertainment of role playing X-rated movies in his leisure time. One of his favorites was one about a female boss catching a male employee in the act with another female employee and threatening to fire them both unless she could join in. Orderly Joe envisioned the adult film while he face pumped the woman on her knees.

"Fuck," he cursed as she gagged on his length. He grabbed hold of the side of her face with both hands and shoved his dick deeper down her throat, just the way he had seen porn stars do in some of the videos he watched.

"Yeah! Swallow this dick for papi," he growled.

He could feel his load building as she licked the spine of his tool and sucked the helmet.

"Come here," Orderly Joe ordered as he lifted her up. She wiped her face and smiled devilishly.

"Turn around and bend over," he commanded.

She did as she was told and grabbed hold of the foot of the metal bed in the empty room. Orderly Joe hiked up the back of her dress. As always, she wasn't wearing any panties. He grabbed his dick and roughly shoved it inside her. She grunted and looked back at him with lust written all over her face as he rabbit fucked her from the back. Orderly Joe applied a death grip on to her hips with his monstrous hands as he savagely thrust his rock hard inside of her. The sounds of clapping could be heard as his pelvis, thighs, and nut sack smacked up against her ass cheeks. Perspiration dripped in between the crack of her ass as it fell from Orderly Joe's face.

"Yeah! Take this dick!"

Orderly Joe pressed down on his sex partner's lower back with his left hand and grabbed a hold of the back of her neck with his right hand. The pressure on her back forced her stomach to press up against the railing of the bed, causing her great discomfort. Just as she was about to order him to stop, Orderly Joe let out a chilling groan. He quickly whipped out his dick and unloaded all over the woman's ass.

"Whew!" he exclaimed.

He was out of breath as he jerked the remainder of his juices on her backside. He smacked her ass with his dick until it was empty. Satisfied, he wasted no time pulling up his scrubs.

"I told you before that I don't like that rough stuff," Nurse Johnson bellowed.

"You know you love that shit." Orderly Joe smiled.

"Fuck you, Joe. You're an asshole," she cursed.

"I don't deny that," he retorted.

Nurse Johnson sucked her teeth. Then, she said, "And, I told you about coming on me like that at work."

"Sorry. Got caught up in the moment." He laughed.

"Yeah. Well, this is not one of your freaking porns, and you're not Mr. Marcus. Now, hand me that sheet."

"I could never be Mr. Marcus. My dick's bigger than his." Orderly Joe grabbed his crotch with one hand and handed Nurse Johnson the bed sheet with the other.

"In your dreams," she dryly remarked.

"I gotta go," Orderly Joe announced, looking at his watch. "Until next time," he said as he made his way to the door.

"Joe," Nurse Johnson called out just as he was about to open the door.

Orderly Joe stopped and turned around. He noticed the awkward look on her face. "What's up?"

Nurse Johnson sighed. Then, she said, "I'm not accusing you of anything." She paused. She was trying to find the right words. "But I hope you're not screwing that girl Baby."

She couldn't figure out any other way to say it, so she used the direct approach. Her words had caught Joe by surprise. He would have never imagined that that was what she had wanted to say to him.

"Mind your goddamn business," he said calmly. "You don't know what the hell you're talking about." Orderly Joe then spun around and exited the room with embarrassment written all over his face.

Chapter 12

Baby peered out of her favorite window and watched as the rain beat against the glass. *It looks as if the sky is about to erupt,* she thought. The trees swayed from side to side and the colors of the clouds changed as they passed. She watched while the sun fought a losing battle to stay up only to slowly but surely fade behind the mountains. Baby listened to the sounds of the wind attacking the window as she waited patiently for who she knew would soon appear. Although they didn't talk about much, their meetings had become a kind of ritual, and she looked forward to them with each day that passed.

"Enjoying the weather?" Treacherous asked.

Baby cut her eyes over at him. Normally, he would just stand or lean on the opposite side of the wall, but, today, she noticed he had pulled up a chair next to her.

"Oh. My bad." Treacherous stood back up, walked over to the table, and returned with a second chair. "For you," he offered.

Treacherous thought he had caught a glimpse of a grin on Baby's face but was unsure. Baby continued to stare out of the window. He tried to read Baby's mood. He noticed how peaceful she seemed as she watched the leaves on the trees do the tango. He decided against striking up a conversation. Instead, he pulled the chair closer to the window and joined her. Treacherous felt a sense of serenity as they watched and listened to the sky pour out its own tears. He leaned back in the chair and took it all in.

"What do you want from me?" Baby asked, looking down at him. The question came out of nowhere. Her voice had trampled over the tranquility in the air. Even she was surprised by her words as they spilled out of her mouth.

"I just want to get to know you." Treacherous's voice was subdued.

"Why?" Baby enjoyed his company but was curious as to why he kept coming around her.

"It's your eyes," Treacherous answered, smiling.

"My eyes?" Baby asked, full of doubt.

"Yeah. Your eyes. They keep calling me over here." Treacherous didn't blink or stutter.

Baby tried fiercely not to fall for his words, but she couldn't help it. He was cute, and she liked him. She couldn't contain the smile that appeared on her face. She turned back to the window to conceal the mood he had put her in.

For the next half hour, Treacherous and Baby remained quiet. Treacherous sat and stared at her with each turn of the page in his magazine. Baby eyed him from the corner of her eye as she continued to enjoy the beauty of the rainfall. She felt comfort in his presence and didn't know why. For the past couple of days, she had felt that way. She turned to Treacherous and exhaled. Baby was the first to break the silence between them.

"Do you believe in fate?"

She had wanted to ask him the question after the first couple of days they had sat and exchanged small talk, but she had not been able to bring herself to. She had felt a connection to Treacherous the first day he had introduced himself to her. Ironically, she didn't want him to think she was crazy despite the fact the two were in a mental institution. Now, here it was a few weeks later, and she had finally built up the nerve to ask.

"I don't know," Treacherous replied, "but I understand what you're feeling."

Baby looked at him with raised eyebrows and asked, "What do you mean?"

"I know how you feel."

"I don't think so."

"No, I do," Treacherous replied.

"It doesn't feel right. I mean, I've barely known you a month and it's like . . . I don't know. I can't explain it. It's like—"

"Like we have a connection," Treacherous stated, finishing her sentence.

Baby nodded her head. Then, she glanced over at him.

Treacherous stared at her. *Her eyes look so sad,* he thought. He could feel her pain, and it reminded him of his own.

Baby was surprised by his words. "I bet you think I'm crazy now, huh?" She chuckled.

"Not at all," he assured her.

"You don't have to say that just to try to make me feel better. I'm a big girl," Baby retorted dryly.

"I'm only saying what I mean," Treacherous shot back.

His answer made Baby blush.

"Have a seat." Treacherous patted the chair next to him. Baby looked from him to the chair. Then, she sat down.

"So, um, why are you in here?" His words came out choppy. He had wanted to ask the question since he had laid eyes on her. Like him, he felt she didn't belong there.

Baby shot Treacherous a look. She wasn't certain if she wanted to tell him. She lowered her head. She became nervous. Treacherous could see the beads of sweat that formed on her forehead. He could tell his question had made her uncomfortable.

"I'm sorry. I didn't mean to—"

"I killed someone," Baby blurted out.

The declaration rolled off her lips so swiftly that Treacherous had barely heard it. "What?"

Baby's eyes shot in his direction. "Fuck. I killed somebody," she repeated.

"That's why I'm here too," Treacherous replied. His straightforwardness caught Baby off guard.

"Don't mock me," Baby spat. She stood up and began to walk away, but Treacherous grabbed hold of her arm.

"I'm for real."

Baby looked into his eyes and sat back down. She could see he wasn't lying.

"So, who did you kill?" he asked with a straight face.

"Who did you kill?" she shot back.

"A kid who was making fun of me and disrespecting me," Treacherous calmly announced. "Your turn. Who did you kill?"

Baby took a deep breath and answered, "My aunt."

"What did she do?"

"Nothing."

"Did y'all have an argument or something?"

Still, Baby did not respond.

"Do you think she deserved it?"

The question caused Baby to squirm in her seat. "No. I don't know. I don't want to talk about it," she answered without looking at him.

Treacherous moved on. "Do you have any brothers or sisters?" Treacherous wanted to know.

"No."

"Me, neither. I know it must've been hard on your parents."

"Mind your business," she lashed out. She stood up for a second time, but she didn't move. She posted back up on the wall and stared out the window.

Treacherous just put his hands up as if to surrender. "You're right." He could see that he had hit a sore spot. "Baby?"

She didn't answer. She had tuned him out. Treacherous moved in closer. He didn't know what to do or say.

"My bad. I didn't mean to upset you," he tried to apologize.

Baby chuckled sarcastically.

"Nah, for real."

Hearing Treacherous's second apology, Baby seemed to relax her shoulders and calm the fire that had begun to brew within her. His voice melted something inside of her. She sank back down into the chair. She looked around the room to see if anyone had seen the miniature scene that she had just put on.

Treacherous moved closer to her. He invaded her space, but she didn't flinch. He was sure she was going to smack him or, at least, tell him to get the hell out of her face, but she did neither. The awkward moment was interrupted by the commotion behind them. Both Treacherous and Baby turned to see what was going on. Apparently, one of the other kids had stolen a page from Baby's playbook. Nurse Johnson and her tray of pills were all over the floor and bottles of water were rolling under the tables.

Baby and Treacherous stared at the scene. Kids were all over the place, stepping on the pills and snatching up water bottles. The sight of Nurse Johnson on the floor and the pandemonium in the room caused Baby to laugh. She threw her head backward and held her stomach. The sight put Treacherous at ease. He joined her in laughter.

The orderlies came running in and ordered everybody to their rooms. Treacherous and Baby stood up. Baby flashed him a warm smile.

"Apology accepted," she said before walking to her room.

From that day on, they were no longer strangers. They were friends.

Chapter 13

Two years later

The banging on the door of his room caused Treacherous to jump out of his sleep. Since he and Baby had been talking, he had been oversleeping. He hadn't had one of his nightmares in months and had been enjoying a good night's sleep despite where he was. His nights consisted of thinking about Baby until he drifted off. His mornings couldn't come quick enough for him. He anticipated the next day when he would see her.

As days turned into weeks and weeks into months, their relationship had progressed. Treacherous felt as if he were reading scenes straight out of his mother's notebooks whenever he was around Baby. Baby's favorite window had actually become their favorite window.

Treacherous's days in the facility got easier and went by faster with Baby as his friend. The more time they spent together, the more they opened up to each other. With only a few months left to go before he reached eighteen, Treacherous explored the strong possibility of life outside of the mental hospital with Baby. He knew once he was released, she would be released seven months later and he was looking forward to that happening. He had no idea where he would go or what he was going to do once he was released, but whatever the case he knew he wanted Baby around.

Treacherous climbed out of bed and dropped to his knees. Once he finished his morning talk with his parents, he hurriedly got dressed.

Treacherous made his way into the dayroom. Aside from the normal operation of the facility, from the television blasting to Nurse Johnson handing out morning medication, something was out of place, and Treacherous immediately picked up on it. Baby was not in their usual meeting spot. Treacherous did another scan of the room. He jumped back when he turned to his left and saw a redheaded girl standing just inches away from his face. He detected the sadness in her facial expression.

"They're taking her away from us," she pouted.

Although she was one of the only kids he and Baby had taken a liking to, he was not in the mood. "Not now, Red," Treacherous said, looking past her. "I'm looking for Baby."

Treacherous noticed Orderly Ron making a beeline over to where he and the redheaded girl stood.

"Red, go back and sit down," Orderly Ron instructed as he approached them. Red flashed her puppy dog eyes at Treacherous. Then, she ran off.

"Ron, you seen Baby?" Treacherous asked before Orderly Ron had the chance to say anything.

"She's in her room," Ron answered. "On quarantine," he added. He looked around as he spoke.

A confused look appeared on Treacherous face.

"Look, Treacherous. You didn't hear this from me." Orderly Ron's voice became low. "The doc's not too happy with you two spending time together like y'all been. Me personally, I don't see anything wrong with it, but Doc said it's setting a bad example for the others." Orderly Ron paused. "So, they're transferring Baby to another facility out in Williamsburg tomorrow morning."

Treacherous couldn't believe his ears. He felt as if he had just been shot in the heart with an arrow. "Are you fucking kidding me?" He kept his voice low to match Orderly Ron's, but his flared nostrils and clenched teeth displayed how angered he was by the news.

"There's nothing you can do about it, Treach." Orderly Ron shook his head empathetically. "Just be happy for the time you guys did have together," Orderly Ron said before making his exit.

Treacherous couldn't think straight. It was if the room was closing in on him. His heart began to ache and an instant migraine came on. "Fuck! This can't be happening," Treacherous cursed.

He banged his right fist into his left palm. The words *there's nothing you can do about it* resonated in his mind as he dragged himself over to his and Baby's favorite window and pulled up a chair. He stared out into the horizon.

There's nothing you can do about it, continued to sound off in his head. Treacherous closed his eyes. All he could think about, at that moment, was never seeing Baby again. The thought infuriated him. He applied pressure to both sides of his head in an attempt to cease the throbbing. *There's nothing you can do about it,* added to the splitting headache. Treacherous jumped up and grabbed hold of the back of the chair he had been sitting in. Then, he flung it across the dayroom. All movement froze, and everyone's attention was drawn to him.

"What the fuck y'all lookin' at?" he barked.

Then, he stormed out of the dayroom. Out of the corner of his eye, he saw movement from Orderly Joe. Treacherous slowed his pace. He wanted to hurt someone, and Orderly Joe was a worthy candidate.

Orderly Joe cracked his knuckles and attempted to approach Treacherous. He was quickly advised by Orderly Ron to stand down. Against his better judgment, he complied.

When Treacherous looked over to his right, he could see Orderly Ron's arm preventing Orderly Joe from coming over to him. *That was the best decision you could have ever made,* Treacherous thought as he exited the dayroom.

Chapter 14

Baby lay on her bunk in tears. She had nearly lost her mind that morning when Orderly Joe told her she was going to be transferred the next day. All she could think about was Treacherous. She imagined the look on his face when he discovered she was gone. *Just when I started to feel safe again, they want to take me away from the only person that makes me feel sane,* she thought.

She had grown accustomed to their talks and longed to hear his low, raspy voice each day. She loved having someone who understood how she felt listen to her. Although there was still so much she hadn't shared with him, she had never felt more comfortable talking to a person. Baby had never felt that way she did around any other person, not even her father, as much as she had loved him. For a while, she had felt dead inside, but Treacherous made her feel alive again. She didn't think she was in love with Treacherous or even loved him, for that matter, but she knew she felt something. She closed her eyes and imagined Treacherous sitting by the window, thumbing through one of the motorcycles magazines he loved reading. She knew she was going to miss the time they spent just sitting and enjoying one another's company. The thought of having that taken away from her angered Baby.

Baby banged her fists on the wall. Then, she rolled over and hopped out of her bunk. She walked over to her door and looked into the hallway. Then, out of nowhere, she turned backward and began kicking on door. The sounds of her kicks echoed down the hallway. She was in the mood for a battle and knew her antics would cause one. As she kicked on the door, she envisioned Orderly Joe being the first on the scene. She pictured herself wrapping her arms around his neck and choking the life out of him before snapping it. As Baby continued her assault on the door, the kicks grew louder, but no one showed up. Baby was surprised. She was sure they would have come running to her room, ready to subdue her.

She screamed hysterically and threw herself onto her bunk. She breathed uncontrollably. A combination of sweat and tears trickled down her face. She knew if she didn't calm down and gain control of her breathing, she would likely pass out. Baby closed her eyes and tried to focus on something relaxing. Surprisingly, an image appeared and caused her to travel back in time to when she was still just an innocent little girl.

Baby waited patiently on the front step. The morning air was chilly, but she didn't care. She busied herself mutilating ants. The small insects were struggling to make their way back to their anthill, which was not far from where she sat. The black, six-legged creatures were in the line of fire and didn't even know it.

"You better hurry up."

Baby's tone was childlike but devilish as she waited for the sound that was music to her ears. The sound stopped her attack on the ant family and caused her to spring to her feet to see if she could see what she had been waiting for.

Baby ran to the end of the black tarred driveway. Although she still couldn't see, she knew it was getting closer.

She walked from the end of the driveway back to the middle and back to the end again. Moments later, the

CBR 750 came to a screeching halt at the beginning of the driveway. Baby beamed with excitement. She watched as the driver put the kickstand down, killed the ignition, and pulled off his helmet.

"What are you doing out here?" He smiled at Baby.

"Waiting on you!"

"Aren't you cold, baby girl?"

"Nope." She smiled.

He lifted Baby into the air, and she laid her head on his shoulder. "You shouldn't be out here this early in the morning in your PJs. I bet your mother doesn't even know you're out here."

Baby just shrugged her shoulders.

"Okay. What do you want to do?"

Baby pointed to her father's bike.

"You wanna ride this early?"

Baby nodded her head excitedly. Her father shook his head and laughed.

"Okay." He quickly gave in.

Baby waited as her father went to retrieve the extra helmet from the garage. He returned and handed it to an ecstatic Baby. She could see her father smiling as she skipped her way to the bike.

After her father helped her climb onto the back of the bike, Baby held on tight as he took off. She always felt like a big girl whenever she rode with her dad. That day, the wind cut into her skin through the thin pajama pants, but she didn't let on to her father that she was cold. She was too busy savoring the moment. Baby and her father rode for what seemed like hours that morning. She lit up when she realized he was pulling into her favorite ice cream parlor.

"Only the best for my baby girl."

Baby's father climbed off the bike and held his hands out to help her off.

The loud bang on her door pulled the plug on her memory. Baby was pissed. The interruption reminded her of how much she had lost. When she looked up, she saw Orderly Joe staring at her through the glass perversely. She shot him a disgusted look.

"You're lucky. Doc told us to ignore your fucking ass," he said just loud enough for her to hear through the crack of the door. "But I got something for you tonight for all that banging you was doing. I'm going to make sure you never forget me when you leave here." Orderly Joe flashed a smile at her. Then, he disappeared.

Baby's skin crawled at his words. She knew what he meant. Right then, she decided there was no way she was going to take her medication that night. She knew the only way she would be able to defend herself was by not being drugged up. Baby promised herself, if and when the time came, she would not go out without a fight.

Chapter 15

Ron's alarm on his watch blared, startling him, causing him to snap out of the doze he had just succumbed to moments earlier. The sound of his motorcycle magazine hitting the floor echoed down the silent hallway. He let out a sigh in frustration. He hated the midnight shift, which was why he usually worked the daytime, but, because he was the one with the least amount of time in at the facility, he had no other choice when he received the call ordering him to come in and cover for one of the other orderlies who had taken ill.

Ron stood up and stretched. It was time to make his hourly suicide watch round. That would be his third of the night. He secured his personal keys to his belt as a reminder for when his shift ended. He was notorious for losing keys. A couple of months ago, he had received a warning for the first set and had gotten written up just the day before for losing a second set. For the life of him, he couldn't figure out where he had misplaced the facility keys, but he knew he had to be extra cautious if he wanted to keep his job. Orderly Ron made his way over to the box on the wall and pulled out the mini flashlight. He shook it to make sure it contained batteries. Then, he clicked it on and off to see if it worked. He took another deep breath and headed down the hallway.

As he made his tour, he shined his flashlight into each of the square glass blocks. For the most part, the kids were either fast asleep or staring up at the cracks in the walls. *It's gonna be a quiet night,* Ron thought. Just then, he noticed something on the floor at the far end of the hallway. The lack of lighting made it difficult for him to make out what it was from where he stood. Not giving it much thought, Ron continued his routine suicide watch tour. He had been fortunate not to have experienced a suicide on his watch.

As he got closer to the second last door on the left side of the hall, he was almost sure he heard a noise. Ron stopped and backed up. He took a second look into the last glass block. The young boy in the room appeared to be sound asleep, so Ron moved along. He pointed the flashlight ahead of him once again, attempting to determine what it was that he had seen on the floor. As he got closer, he realized that it was a liquid of some kind. Instead of checking the last two doors or inspecting the storage closet, Ron hurried his way down the hallway. Once in front of the room, he stared at the liquid with surprise. Ron quickly shined his pen light into the glass block. He was puzzled. He noticed Red wasn't in her bed. Ron stepped back and reached for the key chain attached to his belt. Before he could unhook the keys, he felt a sharp pain to the right side of his head right before his vision became blurred.

Ron crashed into the metal door. The jolt from his body hitting it woke him up just in time for him to attempt to break his fall. He used his left hand to brace himself as he landed in the liquid that lay on the floor in front of the door. The second hit to the head put Ron out completely. His body fell over into the pool of blood and darkness fell upon him.

Treacherous's plan couldn't have gone any smoother. When he first noticed the set of keys lying in the hallway yesterday morning after receiving the disturbing news about Baby, he was convinced it was a sign from God.

The blood in front of room B6 was an unexpected stroke of luck that had added to his execution. Treacherous bent down and grabbed a hold of Orderly Ron's legs. He dragged him down to what was once his own room and opened the door. His adrenaline was in overdrive. Although he had planned this, for the most part, he was now moving off pure instinct.

"Nothin' personal," he whispered to an unconscious Ron.

After relieving Orderly Ron of his keys, Treacherous closed the door behind him and locked it back up. The first part of his mission was complete. Now, it was time for him to move forward with the second part.

Chapter 16

Baby lay still on her bunk. She had just woken up from one of her nightmares. In this one, she wore a pink dress, white socks, and white shoes. It was Sunday, and she was getting ready for Sunday School. Baby could see herself in the bathroom mirror, which was still covered with steam because of the shower she had just taken. She had both arms up as she pulled her hair into a tight ponytail. As the dream advanced, she was no longer alone. A figure appeared behind her. Baby fought to wake herself from the dream but was unable to. The figure had her in his embrace while penetrating her with two middle fingers from behind. Baby attempted to scream, but there was no sound in her dream. She tried to fight the figure off, but she had no strength. The knock on the bathroom door saved her by waking Baby from her dream.

Beads of sweat rolled down her forehead and all down her back. She heard footsteps walking down the hall, and she knew who it was. Baby slowly slid out of bed. She squatted down, walked over by the door, and stood up against the wall. She braced herself as the lock clicked. Baby was determined not to let the monster finish what he had started.

Treacherous moved slowly down the hall. When he reached the door, he peered into the room. To his surprise, the room was empty. Treacherous slid the key into the lock and slowly turned the knob. He stuck his head into the room. Then, he stepped in.

"Baby," he whispered.

"Fucker!" was all Treacherous heard as a gust of wind passed by him. The kick to his leg caused him to reach for his shin while the punch to his chin slightly dazed him.

"Baby, it's me," Treacherous whispered again, moving out of striking distance.

Baby did not hear him. She was too busy throwing punch after punch, missing and landing them all at the same time. Treacherous got up under her and grabbed her by the waist. He body slammed her onto the bed. Then, he forced his weight on top of her.

"Baby! Baby! It's me," he repeated just loud enough for her to hear.

The sound of Treacherous's voice in her ear took Baby by surprise and snapped her out of her blind rage. Her only focus prior was hurting who she thought to be Orderly Joe. A wave of relief swept over her when she realized it was Treacherous. She stopped moving and stared at him. Treacherous released her arms and touched her cheek gently.

"It's me, Baby. I got you," Treacherous said, while staring down at her.

Baby wrapped her arms around Treacherous's neck. She was so happy to see him.

"We gotta get up outta here," he said, pulling her arms from around his neck and standing up. "Come on. Get dressed 'cause we gotta move."

"Where are we going?" Baby asked, hurrying off the bed.

"I don't know, but we gettin' up outta here. Just trust me."

Baby quickly slipped into her jeans and sneakers. Then, she bent down to tie them. Treacherous dropped to his knees and grabbed her face.

"You trust me, don't you?" His voice was soft and rough at the same time.

"I guess," Baby replied.

"No, that's not good enough," he said. "I need to know."

"Yes. For now," Baby retorted with a slight smile on her face.

Both Treacherous and Baby slipped out of the room and down the hall. Baby noticed the blood coming out of Red's room as they passed by.

"Come on." Treacherous knew the sight of the blood bothered Baby but he needed her to stay focused.

Baby and Treacherous raced down the staircase at the far end of the hall, taking two steps at a time. Once at the bottom of the stairs, Treacherous looked out the window. He immediately spotted the exit.

"When we get out here, I need you to go to the left and stand by that gate at the end of the hall. I need to go take care of something real quick. Can you do that?"

Baby just nodded her head.

"Okay, here we go."

Treacherous kissed Baby on her forehead, turned the knob and opened the door. He heard a noise coming from the room directly in front of the stairwell. He turned to Baby, who had apparently heard it too by the expression on her face and the shrug of her shoulders.

Treacherous slid to the right side of the door from where the noise had come from as Baby followed and stood to left. Treacherous cursed to himself because Baby was closest to the door. There was no doubt that whoever was coming through it would see her first. The door swung open and the curly hair of Orderly Joe appeared in the window.

Baby could hear the wheels of the cart rolling toward them. Seconds later, Orderly Joe emerged, walking right past her, pulling the cart into the hall. The mini earbuds and the blaring music coming out of them were a distraction for Joe, making him oblivious to Baby's presence.

Baby intended to take full advantage of the situation. She let Joe enter the hallway. Once he had cleared the entrance, she sprang into action.

Treacherous heard Joe humming to the music as he watched the door close behind him. Treacherous flashed a psychotic smile as Joe's eyes widened with fear when he set them on Treacherous. He was so afraid of Treacherous's presence that he never noticed the true danger he was in.

Baby grabbed hold of the fire extinguisher from off the wall and swung it with all her might. The extinguisher connected with the side of Joe's head. He fell onto the cleaning cart and knocked it over right before he went crashing to the floor. Cleaning supplies went everywhere.

Treacherous watched as Baby followed through with her assault. She stood over Joe, kicking and stomping him intensely as she called him names like "sick muthafucka" and "pervert." Joe curled up into a fetal position. Baby was in a blind rage as she continued to bash Joe's face in with the fire extinguisher. All she could think about at that moment was the violation Orderly Joe had committed against her. With each blow she delivered, images of him touching her flashed in her mind. She switched from Joe's head to his private parts. Orderly Joe lay there motionless. Unbeknownst to her, he had taken one too many hits to the head.

"Baby! Baby!"

The sound of Treacherous's voice snapped her out of her trance. She looked up at him. Then, she looked down at her hands. She could feel the blood on her face as well. It reminded her of why she had been committed to the hospital in the first place.

"Here! Take this," Treacherous said, handing her his T-shirt. "Use that to clean yourself up and go over to that gate and watch out for anyone else. I gotta go handle this."

Baby nodded as she wiped Joe's blood from her face.

Treacherous stepped over Joe's body and headed for his destination. As luck would have it, the doctor's office was unlocked when Treacherous checked the knob. He let himself in and made his way over to the file cabinet. He skimmed through the alphabetized folders. When he reached his and opened it, it was empty. Treacherous became upset instantly. At that moment, he wished Doctor Flannigan was present at the hospital. He wanted to kill him. He was nearly in tears as he thumbed through the file cabinet for a second time, but to no avail. The manila envelope meant everything to him, and he couldn't believe he would have to part with it.

In the midst of his search, he came across Baby's file. He snatched it up and slammed the file cabinet shut. He then turned to make his way out of the office. Out of sheer luck, he spotted what he was looking for on the doctor's desk. His mother's notebooks were sitting on top of the manila envelope along with his file. Treacherous was relieved. He stared at the notebooks and took a deep breath. After scooping them and his file up, he headed for the door. He heard footsteps on the other side just as he reached it.

Baby was leaning on the gate, waiting on Treacherous to return. Her head had begun to hurt, so she closed her eyes in an attempt to slow the pain. As she opened them, she thought she saw a figure at the end of the hall. She blinked in attempt to clear her vision. Once she realized her eyes were not deceiving her, Baby moved to the left then squatted down and waited with anticipation as the figure drew closer. A smile appeared across her face and her headache instantly went away.

Convinced whoever had walked by had moved past the doctor's office, Treacherous slowly opened the door and peered out. He immediately recognized who it was. He didn't, however, see Baby. He knew he had to act fast. It was just a matter of time before the figure discovered Joe's body.

As expected, he heard Nurse Johnson's scream as he made a mad dash down the hall in her direction. Before he could reach her, Baby appeared out of nowhere and silenced her. By the time he got down the hall, Baby had Nurse Johnson on the floor and was straddling her and pounding her in the face. He knew if he didn't stop her, she would beat Nurse Johnson to death. He grabbed Baby by the arm to cease her rage. She turned and gave him an evil stare. Then, she rose to her feet, but not before kicking Nurse Johnson in the midsection.

"That's for not helping me, bitch!" she yelled down at Nurse Johnson. Her words fell on deaf ears. The kick had instantly put Nurse Johnson's lights out.

"Baby, let's get the fuck out of here," Treacherous insisted as he headed for the door.

Baby trailed behind him.

Once outside, Treacherous searched the parking lot for the black Ninja 750 that Orderly Ron had always bragged about. He spotted it parked over in the corner by itself. He and Baby rushed over to the machine and hopped on the bike. He handed Baby the manila envelope along with their files. Then, he retrieved the motorcycle's key from Orderly Ron's key chain. Treacherous started the bike up. The sound was music to his ears.

"You ready?" he asked, looking back at Baby.

"Ready as I'll ever be," she replied.

"Well, let's get the hell out of here then."

He paused and reflected on a particular scene he had read about his parents in his mother's memoirs. For the first time, he truly understood the significance behind his mother's words. Treacherous looked back over at the place that had been keeping him confined for the past couple of years and stuck his middle finger up at it. He smiled when he saw Baby doing the same.

"Hold on tight."

Treacherous popped the bike into gear and yanked the throttle. Baby held on tight as the two of them peeled off into the darkness, leaving the hospital in the distance.

Chapter 17

Mrs. Jazmyne Love had just enjoyed a luxurious bath before rinsing off in a hot, steamy shower. She snatched up her towel and wrapped it around her nudeness. Then, she climbed out of the shower. She wiped the steam away from the mirror. She smiled at what she saw. Her silky, shoulder-length hair belonged in a Maybelline commercial, and her natural 38 Cs could easily be mistaken for implants done by one of the best doctors money could buy in the Dominican Republic.

Jazmyne's flat, flawless mid would make the average young girl jealous and women her age who had given natural birth, like her, envious. It was hard to believe she was the mother of a seventeen-year-old. At the seasoned age of thirty-eight, she was convinced that she could still give any twenty-one-year-old a run for her money and turn the heads of men her age and younger and even women for that matter.

Jazmyne grabbed hold of another towel and wrapped her hair. The sound of what seemed to be the house phone slamming down startled her.

"Honey, what's wrong?" Jazmyne asked her husband, rushing out of the bathroom. The first thing she noticed was the disturbed look on her husband's face.

Arthur Love could not muster up the words to answer his wife. Instead, tears spilled out of his eyes and onto the hardwood floors in the bedroom.

"Sweetheart, who was that on the phone?" Her voice was full of concern.

"The station," Arthur Love managed to reply. He sat on the edge of the bed with his shoulders hunched over, shaking his head like a man who had just been defeated.

"What's wrong? Talk to me." His wife walked over to him. She placed her hands on his back and rubbed it. She knew how he got when it came to his work and wondered what had him so upset.

Arthur continued to shake his head. He was too choked up to spit out the disturbing news.

"Honey, please. You're scaring me."

Jazmyne sat next to her husband and wrapped her arms around him. She hadn't seen him that emotional in quite some time. She knew there weren't too many things in the world that could upset him or make him shed a tear the way he was at that moment. One was his work; the other was his family.

In the eighteen years they had been together and the sixteen they had been married, she had only seen him cry three times: once, when he had killed someone in the line of duty for the first time; the second was out of anger when a criminal had won a case he was guilty of; and the third was out of hurt when he stood in court and felt he had failed their daughter. As the thoughts crossed her mind, an uneasy feeling swept through her body.

"Art, what is it? Tell me!" she demanded.

Arthur Love took a deep breath. "It's Baby!"

Those two simple words nearly took her breath away. Her name hadn't been spoken in their house in over a year because they had agreed that they wouldn't. The sound of her daughter's name raised the hairs on the back of Jazmyne's neck and flooded her eyes with tears. She tried to fight them back, but she couldn't. The floodgate of tears came gushing out of her eyes. Only, her tears were of anger. The memories that came behind hearing her daughter's name flashed through Jazmyne Love's mind at warp speed. A sharp pain jolted through her heart as the images of what had torn their family apart invaded her mind.

"No!" she screamed. "I won't do this again," she said, shaking her head vigorously. "I won't let her destroy what we've managed to repair in this past year."

Arthur Love looked up at his wife and said, "You don't even know what's happened."

"I don't care. And I don't want to know!" she boomed.

Arthur Love sighed. "She's our child," he reasoned.

"I said I don't care!" As far as she was concerned, her child had been buried over a year ago along with all the other memories that came with her.

Arthur Love stood and said, "I have to go."

Jazmyne chuckled with teary eyes. "After all we've been through, all she's put us through and everything we discussed," she cried out, "you're going to just up and run to her aid, just like that?"

Her words tore into her husband's back as he put on his jacket. He shoved his service weapon into the holster and made his way to the door.

"It's not like that," he turned and said.

"So, how is it then, Art?" she asked with her hands on her hips and tears streaming down her face.

"There's been a murder," Arthur Love replied before walking out of the bedroom.

Jazmyne Love stood there, looking dumfounded. The word "murder" resonated in her mind. Despite all that had happened and all the resentment she held for her daughter, the words her husband had just delivered awakened her maternal side. She was stricken with a sense of guilt. She was overwhelmed with mixed emotions and became lightheaded. Jazmyne Love fell to the bedroom floor and began to weep for what she believed to be the loss of her child, knowing the part she had played in the matter.

Chapter 18

Craig Barnes pulled into the local Super 8 motel. He was having a good day. His anticipation level increased by the second, as he filled out the information on the card and submitted his driver's license in order to rent a room.

As soon as Craig exited the office of the motel with the room key in hand, he became more turned on than he had been already, seeing the way the young girl he intended to enjoy sexually sat on his bike.

He rubbed the front of his Levi's jeans at the sight of the young caramel-complexioned girl straddling his Suzuki GSX-R1000. Her miniskirt gave him easy visibility to her purple thong, left ass cheek, and thigh. As she licked her lip gloss—coated lips and twirled her tongue around seductively, his dick stiffened. He knew he was just mere moments away from putting his sex game down on the teenager. It had been a lot of work, he thought, but not enough to make him call it quits. Every hustler up and down Broad Street wanted a piece of the young tenderoni, but it was him she had chosen. Between putting in quality time and spending money, he knew his investment was well worth the wait, especially after he had learned that she was a virgin, which was one of the main reasons he had been so patient. Now, it was all finally about to pay off.

"You sure you ready for this, shawdy?" he asked, with a half smile, flashing his gold tooth.

"I may be young, but I'm ready," she sang like a backup singer for Keith Sweat.

"That's what I'm talking about." Craig rubbed his hands together excitedly. "We right 'round back." He threw one leg over the back of his bike. "You know how to ride one of these things?"

"No," the young girl replied in a sexy tone. "But I can't wait to ride one of these," she said as she scooted back into Craig's crotch area.

Craig smiled again. "Well, I'ma teach you how to ride one of these and one of these, the right way, shawdy," he slyly remarked, pressing his rock hard up against her back.

"I like the sound of that," she cooed.

Craig's motorcycle roared when he started the engine. He took the young girl's hand and placed it on the clutch. Then, he put the bike in gear. Craig guided the young girl's hands on the handlebars as they drove around to the back of the motel. Thoughts of what he intended to do to her invaded his lustful mind as they pulled in front of the door to their room. Craig killed the ignition on his bike and climbed off. Then, he took the young girl by the hand and escorted her to the room. She stood behind him, rubbing her hands along the width of his back while he slid the key card into the door.

"Shit," he cursed.

"What's wrong?" the young girl asked, alarmed.

"Fuckin' key keeps lightin' up red."

"Here. Let me try," she offered, taking the key out of Craig's hand.

The young girl slipped from behind Craig and gained position in front of him. Then, she gently slid the card into the door lock. The sound of a click could be heard as the lock device lit up green.

"Damn, shawdy! You got the magic touch," Craig teased, slipping his hands around the young girl's waist.

"It's all magic, baby," she playfully replied as she opened the door.

"And, I got that magic wand that'll cast a spell on you, too," Craig continued.

He wrapped his arms around her and kissed her on the side of the neck as he followed her into the room. She could feel his weight on her 115-pound frame as he continued to smother her with a bear hug.

"Damn, baby! You're heavy." She giggled.

Before she could tell him to release her, his entire weight of his body came crashing down on her, sending them both straight to the floor.

"What the fuck, nigga!" she yelled, trying to free herself from under him, attempting to push him up off of her.

"Get the hell—"

That was as far as she got with her words before her own body became limp.

Chapter 19

The sign read RICHMOND CITY LIMITS as Treacherous cruised up the dark and empty lane of Interstate 95 northbound with no particular destination in mind. Baby hugged him tightly around the mid with the manila envelope safely in between them. The city of Richmond glowed to their left as the cool summer breeze offered a new chill complimentary of the water off to their right. Treacherous's adrenaline was still pumping full speed from all of the excitement back at the mental hospital. His eyes had been watering since he had jumped on the highway from the gust of continuous wind smacking him square in the face as he traveled up the interstate. Despite his vision being blurry from the wind, something inside of him told him to keep going, so he rode solely off of pure instinct. He had no idea how long he had been driving, but it felt as if it had been all night.

Baby's ponytail blew in the wind as she stared at her city, while deep in thought. The scene put her in the mind of one of her favorite movies with Nia Long and Larenz Tate as Treacherous navigated the bike through her hometown. It had been quite some time since she had been so close to home, and, at that moment, she realized just how much she had missed it. The familiar sign for the Chamberlain Street exit reminded her of some of her wild and fun times at the Virginia Union parties and the football games she had attended. Baby closed her eyes and laid her head on Treacherous's back as she tightened her grip. Thanks to him, she was able to breathe again. She thought it would be a long time before that would ever happen again and she was grateful.

Treacherous could feel the warmth of Baby's face pressed against his back. He placed his left hand on top of the back of hers as he navigated the motorcycle with the right. He gave her an assuring rub. He had no regrets about what he had just done nor did he have any remorse. During their breakout, all he could think about was how his father would have handled the situation had it been his mother in Baby's predicament.

At seventeen and with only a few more months to go before he was released and Baby being seven months younger than he was, there was no way he was going to allow her to be transferred to another facility and have to get through her stay without him. From day one, when they first laid eyes on one another officially, in his mind and in his heart, he knew she was the one, and he knew he was rescuing them both. As the days had passed and he learned more and more about Baby, he knew he had found in her what his father had found in his mother: a ride or die chick.

Treacherous's chain of thought was broken when Baby tapped him on the side. She pointed up ahead for Treacherous to get off at the next exit. He nodded and accelerated the motorcycle. Treacherous veered off onto the exit that read 60–67. Baby directed him to the back of the motel on Midlothian Turnpike, and then instructed Treacherous to park the bike up under a set of bushes. The tree served its purpose as a camouflage in the semi-dark parking lot.

"This is where the so-called ballers come to trick," Baby informed Treacherous, referring to the motel.

Treacherous gave her an odd look.

"This is where the drug dealers come to fuck chicken-heads and sack chasers," she said, rephrasing her statement.

Treacherous smirked at her bluntness.

"We should be able to find a place to stay here for the night," Baby said matter-of-factly.

"How? You got friends who come here?"

Baby laughed. "No, silly." She shook her head at how naïve Treacherous was. "You ever rob anybody, Treach?"

Her question embarrassed Treacherous. Not because he didn't know what she was talking about but because he had come from a long line of robbers, and yet he had never experienced the act. "No, but I will," he boldly stated.

"Good." Baby smiled. "Because you are."

Now, it was Treacherous's turn to laugh.

"I'm glad you find it funny, but I'm serious." Baby was stone-faced. "Now, here's what we're gonna do. . . ."

Chapter 20

Craig opened his eyes, but he couldn't see a thing. Everything was a blur, and he had a splitting headache, but he didn't know why. His shoulders were sore, and the tingling sensation in his legs let him know that they were asleep. Craig tried to rise up, but he soon discovered that he did not have the usage of his hands or legs.

"What the hell?" he cursed.

A sense of fear and confusion set in as he struggled to lift himself from what he knew to be a bed.

"What the fuck is this shit?" he bellowed, realizing his hands had been tied behind his back. His feet were also tied together.

"Shut the fuck up," a baritone voice boomed in his ear right before a blow was delivered to the side of his head with what Craig believed to be the butt of a gun.

Craig tried to fight off the pain caused by the assault, but there was no way he could stop the blood from pouring out of the gash on the side of his head. The injury only added to the imminent danger he knew he was in. As he regained his senses, it all came back to him. The last thing he remembered was following the young girl into the room after she had gotten the door to open. Next, he felt a sharp pain in the back of his head before everything went completely black.

Craig clenched his teeth at the thought of getting caught slipping. Then, his thoughts immediately zeroed in on the young girl. "Bitch, you muthafuckin' set me up."

"No, Craig—" the young girl tried to plead before being cut off.

"Both y'all shut the fuck up," another female demanded.

Craig silently cursed himself for being lured in by a piece of ass. After he had quickly come to the realization, his only other thought was how he could make it out of the situation alive.

"Yo! Whoever you are, we don't gotta go through this," he started to reason. "I got money, and I'll take you to it if you let me go."

"We don't want your money," Craig heard the male voice say.

Instant fear overcame him. He immediately began backtracking, trying to figure who he had done wrong and who he had been beefing with, old and new. If they were not there for money, then he was sure they were there to take his life.

Craig strained to open his eyes. Drops of blood spilled into his right eye, making it difficult to see out of it, but he managed to get his left one to focus. The first sight he laid eyes on was the young girl balled up in a fetal position against the wall with her mouth, hands and feet gagged and bound. She, too, was bleeding from her head, and fear was plastered across her face. The sight confused him. With his good eye, he did a quick scan of the room.

Next, his eye landed on a female standing near the bathroom. She was not too far from where the young girl sat in bondage on the floor. She did not look familiar to him, so he nixed the possibility of the situation being over a female. He was surprised to see that she did not have a mask or anything on to disguise her identity. Where he came from, that was a bad sign.

He noticed the revolver he kept tucked in his ankle in her right hand along with a thick tree branch in her left one and wondered if she was the one who had cold cocked him in the back of the head. His eye roamed the room further, but he could not locate a face to go with the male voice he had heard. He wondered if he, too, did not have anything concealing his identity. His question was quickly answered.

"You lookin' for me, chump?" Treacherous came from around the other side of the bed and stood in front of Craig.

Craig struggled to look up at Treacherous. Nothing about Treacherous rang a bell with him. Despite his size, Craig could see that he was a young kid. He couldn't help but laugh to himself. He knew there was no way Treacherous could possibly know who he was.

"Yo, dawg," he said calmly. "This is all just one big misunderstanding. Now, I know you don't know who I am because, if you did, you wouldn't be standing here right now, which is why I have a proposition for you. So, here's how we can handle this." Craig paused. Then, he said, "I got about three grand in my pocket. Why don't you and your little girlfriend just take that and disappear, and I'll forget this ever happened. I give you my word, and my word is everything in these streets."

"Well, you're right about two things," Treacherous began. "One, I don't know who you are; and two, all together you had $2,864 in your pocket, not including what your chain, watch, and bracelet are worth. I left the change, though. All that other shit you talkin' is for the birds," Treacherous firmly stated.

Craig laughed to himself. He had underestimated Treacherous. He hadn't even realized he had been relieved of his jewelry. "So, what do you want then?" He wanted to know.

"It's nothin' personal," Treacherous offered. "You were just in the wrong place at the wrong time. We just needed a place to lay our heads for the night and a couple dollars to hold us over."

"You must be fuckin' kiddin' me." Craig laughed. "I'm being jacked by a couple of homeless runaway kids."

"Babe, stop talkin' to that fuckin' pedophile," Baby barked, taking offense to Craig's last statement.

"Pedophile? Naw, shawdy, that ain't on my jacket," Craig said in his own defense.

"Oh, no. So, what do you call bringin' a sixteen-year-old girl to the motel to fuck, you dirty dick muthafucka?" Baby lashed out.

"Shawdy, I don't know where you from, but in the State of Virginia, she legal, so she a consenting adult."

Had he known how Baby was going to react to his statement, he would have thought before he spoke. Before anyone knew what was happening, Baby snatched the gun out of Treacherous's hand, grabbed one of the pillows off of the bed and, using the pillow as a silencer, shot Craig in the groin. Before Craig's screams could be heard, Baby took the pillow and suffocated him. Treacherous stood there in shock. Everything happened so fast. He couldn't believe Baby's actions. The young girl's muffled cries could be heard as she sat in the corner, wide-eyed and soiling the carpet.

"Treach, shut that bitch up!" Baby commanded, as she continued smothering Craig.

Treacherous wasted no time. He walked over to the young girl. The sight of the gun he had earlier relieved from Craig's waistband caused her to go silent as he stood in front of her with the weapon down by his side. She looked as if her eyes would jump out of their sockets at any moment.

Baby released the pillow from Craig's face. She was confident that she had snuffed all the life out of him. The entire time she was smothering him, all she could think of was how Craig reminded her of the type of people who took advantage of the weak and helpless. Images of her own past ordeal played in her mind until she no longer saw Craig's face but rather another.

She removed the pillow, and all was confirmed. Craig's lifeless eyes peered up at her. The first time she had killed, she felt nothing, and this time was no different. She had no remorse for what she had done, and, in her mind, she had just done the world a big favor. Baby tossed the pillow to the side.

"There's been a change of plans. We can't stay here. We gotta go," Baby announced.

Treacherous nodded in agreement.

"You know we can't leave her here like this," Baby said. "She knows what we look like."

Treacherous didn't say anything. He had already thought the same thing. Instead, he gave Baby a confirming look. The young girl sat with tears streaming down her face, shaking her head, but Baby and Treacherous paid her no mind.

"You sure you can handle it?" Baby asked all too prepared to finish what she had started. She knew Treacherous had killed before, but she knew that her first kill had been intentional and his had not.

Rather than answer her, Treacherous walked over to the bed, grabbed another pillow and walked back over to the young girl. He, too, felt nothing as he and the young girl's eyes connected right before he placed the pillow over her face. The feathers of the pillow floated in the air as smoke lingered around the hole the bullet had caused. The shot painted a maroon picture behind the young girl's head as her brain matter decorated the wall. Treacherous dropped the pillow to the floor. The bullet from the .38 revolver made it appear as if the young girl had a third eye.

"It had to be done," Baby told him.

"I know."

Baby smiled. At that moment, she knew no matter what, regardless of how dangerous or extreme, she would go to hell and back with Treacherous and for him.

"Okay, let's get out of here," she said.

After checking to see if the coast was clear, one by one, Treacherous and Baby exited the room. Baby stopped next to Craig's bike. Treacherous turned around, realizing she was not behind him. She flashed the keys to Craig's motorcycle.

"You know how to ride?" Treacherous asked her.

She smiled and hopped on the bike. The next sound that was heard was Baby's new bike roaring. She revved the engine and said, "Follow me."

Treacherous jogged over to the bike they had ridden in on and started it up. Side by side they whizzed out of the Super 8 motel parking lot and back on to Interstate 95.

Chapter 21

"Goddamn it," Andre Randle cursed as he tripped over an object on his living room floor and stumbled into his two-bedroom home. He used the wall to catch his balance. He slid his hand along it in search of the light switch. Moments later, his living room was illuminated. The first thing he saw was the object that had nearly caused him to fall.

"Goal!" he yelled as he kicked his shoe over into the corner like a professional football punter. After nearly losing his balance for a second time, Andre staggered over to the couch and plopped all 212 pounds of him onto it. It was a miracle he had made it home in one piece after throwing back six shots of tequila and four Budweisers at the local bar. Since he had retired, every night had been a miracle for him. He chuckled at the thought of being pulled over by a police officer and asked to take a sobriety test or, even worse, charged with DUI.

Andre reached underneath himself and retrieved the remote control that had poked him in his rear the moment he sat down and turned on his sixty-inch flat screen. His five-year-old black-and-white terrier named Mutt came waddling out of the kitchen and jumped up on the sofa and found a resting spot next to the ex-chief. Andre flicked through the television channels until he found a local news station. Then, he got up and made his way to the kitchen.

He pulled out the pitcher of water from the fridge and drank nearly half of the water out of the container, stopping only when he got a brain freeze. He, then, grabbed the two remaining slices of pepperoni pizza out of the Papa John's box, slapped them on a plate, and tossed them into the microwave. Andre leaned over on the kitchen counter and grabbed hold of his head as the pizza warmed. There was no doubt in his mind that he was going to have a splitting headache in the morning. The beeping sound of the microwave woke him out of his brief nod. He took a bite of one of the slices. Then, he made his way back over to the sofa.

"Anything interesting happen, boy?" he asked Mutt before he turned his attention to the television.

The background of the reporter caught Andre's eye and caused him to increase the volume.

"Richmond authorities are working on getting us photos of the two patients. No word, as of yet, as to why they acted out so violently before their escape, but we will bring you more details as this story unfolds."

"Christ, just what we need, more crazy muthafuckas on the loose," Andre said out loud. He laughed at his own joke and switched the channel.

Chapter 22

Treacherous stepped out of the bathroom with a towel wrapped around his waist. He used a second towel to wipe the water from his newly clean-shaven head. *A shower was just what the doctor ordered,* he thought, feeling refreshed after all that had happened. The motel was far from a five-star establishment, but it served its purpose. He and Baby were able to find a place to lay their heads and take hot showers for as long as their money allowed without needing any ID and no questions asked.

Although he had no remorse, the incident was still fresh in his mind. He was unaware of the amount of blood that had sprayed on him until he watched it run off his body and disappear down the drain. Treacherous couldn't wait to put on a pair of the brand new boxer briefs, one of the wife beaters, and one of the outfits he had purchased during his and Baby's stop at Walmart before they checked into the motel. Walmart wasn't his preferred place to shop, but, under the circumstances, he knew his options were limited. Besides, the outfits he had copped there were an improvement from the hand-me-down clothes he was forced to wear at the mental hospital.

"That felt good," he announced, snatching the hand towel off his head.

Baby didn't answer. She was too engrossed in what she was doing. She lay stretched out across one of the double beds on her stomach with her legs crossed in the air. She was wearing a white tee, and she was reading.

"What the hell you doin'?" Treacherous asked, snatching the notebooks and envelope away from her.

"What the fuck is wrong with you?" she asked. His reaction had surprised her.

"Why you reading my shit?" His words were strong. She could tell he was upset.

"I didn't think you'd mind," Baby offered. "I . . . I'm sorry." She knew what it was like to be violated by another or have one's privacy invaded. She instantly regretted her decision.

Her apology calmed Treacherous, and he felt bad. Seeing Baby lying there, reading his mother's notebooks, had caught him off guard, and he'd reacted without thinking. "It's okay," he retorted, putting the notebooks back into the manila envelope.

"I really am sorry. I didn't—"

"I said it's cool," Treacherous assured her.

Baby caught his signature grin and knew everything was fine. She also caught the rips and indentions in his midriff. Baby couldn't take her eyes off of Treacherous's handsome physique. He was cut and had muscles everywhere. Baby was an arms woman, but she admired the fact that Treacherous had the total package. She liked the way his traps sat behind but just above his broad shoulder blades, while his chest was thick and stood at attention like he was in the military. She couldn't help but watch as beads of water slid down his chest and eight pack like a slide on a playground. The sight had Baby mesmerized as the water danced its way down Treacherous's abs until landing on the top of his towel.

"Huh?" Treacherous's voice broke the spell the water and his abs had momentarily cast on Baby.

"I said what's wrong with you?" Treacherous repeated.

"Nothing." She shook her head. "I need a shower," she added, rolling over and off the bed.

Treacherous couldn't help but notice how firm Baby's inner thighs were. The hiking of the tee gave him a full view between her legs and a partial view of her ass cheeks. The gap between them allowed him to see straight to the bathroom. Treacherous watched in awe as Baby's firm cheeks bounced underneath the tee one after the other. When she reached the bathroom door, Baby spun around. Treacherous turned his head and looked around the room at nothing in particular. She walked back over to him.

"I should've asked," Baby said, placing her hand on Treacherous's arm. "You'll never have to worry about something like that again." She moved her hand up to the side of his face. "I promise."

"I believe you." Treacherous stared into her eyes. He could see the truth all in them.

Baby slid her hand from Treacherous's face down to his chest and leaned in. She kissed Treacherous on the cheek. Then, she made her way to the shower. Treacherous turned and watched for a second time as Baby sashayed her way to the bathroom. The front of his towel rose as his dick stiffened from the sight. He sat on the bed and ran his hand across his smooth head. He let it run down his face as a glimpse of his life flashed before his eyes. He was unsure of what the future held for him, but he knew he was sure of one thing: he wanted it to include Baby.

Chapter 23

Jazmyne Love stood in front of her sister's gravesite and pulled off her Dior sunglasses. She bent down. Then, she took the bouquet of flowers she held in her hand and placed them in front of the tombstone. It had been nearly six months since she had visited the site. A sense of guilt swept through her. She couldn't believe she had allowed so much time to elapse. Had it not been for the mentioning of her daughter's name, Jazmyne knew she would not have come to Jazelle's grave and had no clue as to how much more time would have passed before she came and paid her respects.

The thought of it caused Jazmyne to resent her daughter even more. It was because of her daughter that her sister was no longer alive. It had been over two years, and Jazmyne had not come to terms with the whole ordeal yet. The incident was still fresh in her mind. It was the memory that kept her up at night and in tears for the first four months after her sister's death. She was still trying to convince herself that there was nothing she could have done to prevent it and that it was not her fault. Tears rolled down Jazmyne Love's face, staining her perfectly applied makeup. She rummaged through her clutch and pulled out a handkerchief.

"Hey, Jaz," she spoke through sniffles. She dabbed her face with the handkerchief. "I know it's been awhile, and you're probably mad at me. I'm sorry." She paused. "I am so sorry," she repeated, "for everything." She shook her head and became choked up. Then, she cleared her throat and said, "I still can't believe you're gone. If I could turn back the hands of time, there's nothing else in the world that I would want to redo other than bring you back and . . ."

Jazmyne put her head down. She cleared her throat for the second time and said, "Anyway, none of this should have ever happened. I miss you so much. I can't believe that little bitch took you from me." Jazmyne's pressure began to rise. "If it weren't for Art, I would've pressed for the death penalty for her ass, daughter or not." Jazmyne tried to calm herself. "Now, her ass is running around on the loose, and there's no telling what she may do next." The thought gave Jazmyne an eerie feeling.

"Even though you were my little sister, you always had my back, right, wrong, or indifferent, no matter what, and I should've had yours. I've asked myself over and over why I didn't react sooner or why I didn't see it coming. I guess I was in denial." Jazmyne closed her eyes tightly. "Please forgive me," she cried. "None of this should have ever happened," she repeated. Jazmyne pressed two fingers to her lips and kissed them. Then, she touched the top of her sister's tombstone. "I love you, sis. I have to go."

Jazmyne Love spun around and walked back to her car just as the levies of her eyes broke and flooded her face.

Chapter 24

A week later

"You sure this is where you saw him?" Treacherous asked Baby as the two of them sat on the latest bike they had jacked.

"I'm positive," Baby replied.

"And you sure it was him?"

"Nigga, in all the time you've known me, have you ever seen me wear glasses?"

Treacherous laughed. He had become used to her smart remarks and sarcasm in the time they had been rolling and living together.

"Not that I can remember," he answered. He knew what was to follow.

"Well, then, you know my vision is perfect."

"One day, your smart mouth is going to get you hurt." Treacherous laughed, shaking his head.

"And you're going to kill the muthafucka who hurt me," she shot back.

He looked back at her.

"What? I said something wrong?"

"Not at all." Treacherous smiled.

"Look." Baby pointed.

When Treacherous turned around and saw the person Baby was pointing at, his eyes grew cold. He couldn't believe his luck. The last time he had seen this person the terms were different and the situation had left a bad taste in his mouth. Now, all bets were off, and the only thing that stood in the way of him settling the score was the air he breathed.

Baby had told him how the house down the street from North Jackson Ward housing projects was in a known drug area and rough neighborhood, but that didn't mean anything to Treacherous. If a drug house was where he would have to get his revenge for the disrespect the person had displayed the last time they laid eyes on each other, then so be it. There was no way he was going to pass up the opportunity.

"Told you." Baby nudged him.

"I never doubted you."

"You want to wait until he comes out, or you want to go up in there?" Baby asked.

"We not waitin' on nothin'," Treacherous replied. His temperature had already begun to rise. "We goin' up in there."

"Whatever you want to do," Baby replied.

"Yeah, that's exactly what I wanna do," Treacherous said, hopping off the motorcycle.

"Man, T-Bop, all the retarded be comin' up outta you when you hit that shit," Doug joked as he watched his get high partner take a hit of the crack he had just purchased from their connect up the block.

"Fuck you, nigga," T-Bop stammered. His mouth twitched as he spoke. The drug had already taken effect. He used to stutter when he was nervous, but he had overcome that long ago. Now, he only stuttered when he got high.

T-Bop took another hit of the pipe. Doug laughed at his friend's reply as he always did. The two had been friends since they were kids. They went back as far as quarter waters and grilled government cheese sandwiches when they both lived in the projects. Their mothers had been get high partners. Doug meant no harm with his joke, and he knew T-Bop knew that. When they were younger, it was Doug who had actually defended T-Bop when the other kids picked on him for being in remedial classes and stuttering occasionally.

The euphoric feeling of the narcotics caused T-Bop to lean back on the sofa and look up to the ceiling. He smiled as images of him as a kid before the drugs played on the wall of the apartment.

"Hey, T! Hey, Momma!" T-Bop laughed as he waved at himself and his mother on the ceiling. He watched as she fixed his favorite blue bowtie. She had made him wear it to school every Monday. Then, she would give him a hug as the school bus driver waited and the kids on the bus all laughed.

The scene changed from T-Bop standing in front of the bus to him standing in front of the judge at age thirteen while his mother stood in the background. Her hair was wild. Her eyes resembled a raccoon's, and her clothes were dingy. She pleaded with the courts not to take her child away from her. As always, the scene brought tears to T-Bop's eyes.

"No! Please!" T-Bop yelled out.

He covered his face to prevent himself from watching the scene any longer. He buried his face in his hands and shook his head. The drug had him bugging. T-Bop's smile returned. He was where he wanted to be: high. That feeling immediately faded when the unexpected impact of the blow to his face caught him by surprise.

"What the hell!" he bellowed, grabbing hold of his head.

He sat up, erect and alert. The blow was enough to sober him up. When he opened his eyes, he saw the male figure with a gun pointed at his face, while a female had

Doug on his knees with one pointed to the back of his head.

"What the fuck is going on?" T-Bop stuttered, still rubbing the spot on his head where he was assaulted.

"Read any good magazines lately?" Treacherous asked rather than answering T-Bop's question.

A confused look appeared on T-Bop's face.

"Remember us?" Baby asked T-Bop.

"Naw," he answered quickly. Ever since he had started getting high, he didn't remember much of anything.

"Sure you do," Treacherous stated. "How could you forget somebody you used to like and somebody you used to disrespect?"

T-Bop had no clue what Treacherous was talking about, but, at that point, he had nearly sobered up completely. He looked back and forth from Treacherous to Baby. The familiarity slowly set in.

"Treach? Baby?"

"I knew you weren't that slow, nigga," Treacherous slyly remarked. Baby remained stone-faced.

"Man, what are y'all doin' here?" T-Bop hadn't felt that nervous since he was in grade school, long before he had taken on a life of crime. Treacherous's earlier statement now made sense to him.

"Don't get stupid on me now, Tony," Treacherous said, calling T-Bop by his birth name.

He reflected on the last time he had seen Treacherous and Baby, when they were all residents at the mental hospital. He remembered the day he had tried to play Treacherous out in front of Baby over the magazine because he had liked Baby. He instantly regretted it, seeing the predicament he was now faced with, especially after recalling what they had done to the orderlies and a nurse at the hospital before they broke out. Beads of sweat formed on Tony's forehead.

"Man, I didn't mean no disrespect back then. I was sick!" Tony stuttered, pleading his case.

"I'm sure you were," Baby snarled.

"Yo, T-Bop, what the fuck is going on, dawg?" a confused Doug asked. He, too, had sobered up behind the fact that he was on his knees with a gun pointed to the back of his head.

"Shut the fuck up," Baby said as she gave him a warning nudge in the back of the head with her revolver. Baby was growing tired of the situation and was ready to go. Out of nowhere, she began to sweat.

"What can I do to make this right?" T-Bop asked, directing his question to Treacherous.

Treacherous shook his head and smirked. "You wanna know what you can do?"

T-Bop nodded his head rapidly.

"You can start by apologizing to me and my girl," Treacherous offered.

"Yo! I'm fuckin' sorry! I swear to freakin' God! I'm sorry!" T-Bop exclaimed. His hands were now folded in a prayer position.

"You should be, muthafucka!" Treacherous rushed over to the couch and was on top of Tony with his .38 shoved in his mouth. He had to hold his breath because of the foul odor that reeked from Tony. A combination of piss, bad breath, musk, and drug residue assaulted Treacherous's nostrils. Tony's eyes resembled that of a goldfish as he begged for his life inaudibly.

"Shut your bitch ass up," Treacherous growled, shoving the barrel deeper into Tony's mouth.

"Damn, man! Don't kill 'im," Doug pleaded for his friend.

"I told you to shut the fuck up!" Baby roared.

She let loose a thunderous shot into the back of Doug's head. Doug's body fell forward to the floor. Tony cried out as loud as he could as he made a failed attempt to push Treacherous up off of him, but the bullet Treacherous force fed him ceased all movement.

"You picked the wrong chick to like, mu'fucka."

Treacherous spit in Tony's face. As he rose up, he let off another round into Tony's chest as an extra precaution.

"Babe, you a'ight?" Treacherous asked Baby as he stepped over Doug's body. Baby dripped with perspiration despite the cool temperature of the crack house.

"Yeah, I'm okay," she answered, wiping her brow. "I just feel a little lightheaded. That's all. This place stinks like shit."

"A'ight. Let's get the hell outta here."

To make his way out, Treacherous retraced his steps, but the loud thud behind him caused him to stop in his tracks. When he turned around, his heart skipped a beat at the sight of Baby lying on the floor.

Chapter 25

The pit of Detective Love's stomach bubbled as soon as he stepped through the door of the gloomy residence. He didn't know how long he would be able to hold his breakfast down. He thought he was going to be sick. Lately, bodies were popping up in the section of Richmond that Detective Love covered, and he dreaded the crime scenes. He had not been lucky enough to keep his lunch down at the scene of the other homicide case he was still working on. He had been investigating the deaths of a thirty-four-year-old man and a sixteen-year-old girl at a Super 8 motel when he received a call about two more homicides.

The smell of the two bodies made him hurl. After six years in homicide, he still had not gotten used to the smell of death. He pulled out his handkerchief and covered his nostrils and mouth to minimize the stench of the foul odor that smacked him in the face like the wife of a cheating husband. Not only had he been exposed to the stench of death at eight a.m. but also the combination of feces, urine, and bad hygiene. The room was flooded with officers who were collecting anything that could be considered evidence. He pulled out a pair of rubber gloves and walked over to one of the other detectives on the scene who was taking notes.

"What do we got, George?" Detective Love mumbled through his handkerchief.

"Hey, Art." Detective George Parks turned and greeted him. "Two victims. One shot to the back of the head, execution style." He pointed to the dead body lying on the floor. "This one," he said, shifting back around and pointing to the body in front of him. "One entry shot through the mouth. A second shot in the chest. Judging by the way they were murdered, I'd say this one here was the intended victim and that guy back there was just a casualty, my theory," Detective Parks concluded.

"Why would you think that?" Detective Love wanted to know.

"No sign of any struggle with that guy there. He was on his knees when the perp killed him. Found a pair of boot prints directly behind his body. He was kneeling before he fell forward from the shot, but this guy here," Detective Parks said, and leaned in, "someone was upset with him. Look here."

Detective Love moved in closer.

"You see how his two front teeth are chipped, and the boot prints come all the way up to the couch?"

"Yeah, which means the perp had to climb on top of the victim and shoved the gun in his mouth before he shot him," Detective Love offered.

"Exactly!" Detective Parks chimed in. "And there was no need for a second shot because the first one had already done the job."

"Makes sense," Detective Love agreed.

"It gets better," Detective Parks added. "I also found traces of dried saliva in the victim's right eye, which means one of the perps had to have spat in the victim's face. Now, it doesn't get any more personal than that."

Detective Parks threw up his hands as if he had just won a title match fight. Detective Love shook his head and smiled. By then, he was immune to the smell which had seeped through his handkerchief.

"You sent the saliva to ballistics?"

"It's en route as we speak."

"So, what were these guys? A couple of petty dealers or something?" Detective Love asked.

"The total opposite."

"What do you mean?"

"They were addicts," Detective Parks answered.

"Jeez! These kids can't be no more than eighteen."

"You hit it right on the head. Both of them."

"Wow! So, some local dealers ran up in here and killed them for the couple of dollars they probably owed," Detective Love surmised.

"Maybe." Detective Parks shrugged.

"You ID 'em, yet?"

"Guy on the floor's name is Douglas Smith. He's been in and out of the system since thirteen, started out in juvie, caught a bunch of misdemeanors and a couple of felonies as an adult, few county bids, nothing serious." Detective Parks paused. Then, he said, "This guy's name is Anthony Morris; got nothing on him, though, as a juvenile or adult, other than being a fucking nutcase." Detective Parks snickered.

"What do you mean by that?" a confused Detective Love asked.

"According to his file, he's been in and out of mental hospitals since he was born."

"For what?"

"Come on, Love. I'm a detective, not a damn doctor." Detective Parks laughed. "I don't remember that shit. I just know, based on what I was told, the kid was all screwed up in the head and was one sandwich short of a picnic basket."

The statement was meant as a joke, but Detective Love found no humor in his colleague's words. Instead, he thought about his own child and how she too had been in a mental hospital up until recently. He was still trying to digest the phone call he had gotten about his daughter killing a man and breaking out of the facility with another patient. He immediately removed the thought and refocused on the reason he was at the house in the first place.

"Let me know if you come up with anything else, and keep me posted on the results from ballistics."

"Will do," Detective Parks replied.

Detective Love turned and headed for the exit.

"Excuse me, Officer," he said to one of his colleagues who was kneeling down, blocking the doorway.

"Oh, sorry about that, sir," the officer said, looking back.

"Whatcha got there?" Detective Love asked.

"That's what I was trying to figure out," the officer replied. "Judging by the looks of these footprints and this clear spot, it looks like another body could have been lying here or something and may have been carried out."

Detective Love kneeled beside the officer and took a closer look. He could see how the officer could have drawn his conclusion. "You might be right, Officer," he agreed as he studied the patterns on the floor.

"Parks, I think we got something," he yelled behind him. "Good work, Bronson," he said, scanning the officer's name tag. "Damn good work."

Chapter 26

Treacherous entered their room carrying a tray and made his way over to where Baby lay. Baby's face glistened with perspiration as she slept. Treacherous stood over her and stared in admiration as she tossed and turned in her sleep the way she had been doing for the past week. He respected the fact that she had been fighting off the medication she had been taking at the asylum before they left. It never dawned on him until then that she was addicted to the drugs they had been feeding her. For him, it was different because he had only taken a mild med, but, for Baby, it was a little more difficult because she had been prescribed something much stronger.

For the first couple of days, Treacherous tried numerous times to persuade her to take some over-the-counter pills, but she refused. He felt helpless as he watched her body shut down. Each day, she grew sicker and sicker. It took all of his being to obey her wishes and not force some painkillers down her throat after she had gone into convulsions and collapsed in the bathroom. She begged him to trust her, and he did. For days, Treacherous watched as her body went through withdrawal. After a few days, her radiant complexion was replaced with a dull beige color, and she had become so weak that he had to feed her broth every day because it was the only thing she could keep on her stomach without vomiting. He could literally smell the medication seeping through her pores.

Treacherous sat next to Baby on the bed and gently dabbed her forehead with a cool, damp rag. He noticed that her skin color was returning to its normal tone. Baby's eyes opened, and a smile appeared across her face the way it always did when she saw Treacherous sitting next to her.

"How you feelin'?"

"Better," she whispered.

"You're lookin' better," Treacherous complimented her as he moved the rag down to her neck.

His words caused Baby's eyes to match the smile she had already had on her face. She raised her arm and placed her hand on top of his. She looked into Treacherous's eyes.

"You ready to eat?" Treacherous asked, breaking the stare. He didn't know why, but he always became nervous whenever Baby looked at him the way she just had.

Baby sat up.

"I bought your favorite: tomato." He flashed a half of a grin as she frowned. He knew she was tired of eating soup, so he always made the same joke to soften her disdain for the liquid food.

Treacherous raised the spoon and blew on the hot soup. Then, he placed his hand underneath it and put it to Baby's mouth.

"I can do it," Baby announced as she took the first spoonful of soup in.

"You sure?"

He had become accustomed to feeding her but was pleased to hear that she felt strong enough to feed herself. Baby nodded her head. Treacherous took the tray and laid it across her lap as Baby held the spoon. For a second, she just stared into the bowl.

"Babe, you sure you got it?" Treacherous asked with uncertainty in his voice.

Baby looked up at him and rolled her eyes. His doubt became her motivation. All in one motion, she raised the spoon and shoved it in her mouth.

"Fuck!" she cried out, dropping the spoon. The soup had burned her tongue.

"That's what you get for tryin'a be all tough and fast." Treacherous chuckled.

"Forget you." She tried to give Treacherous attitude, but the smile wanting to burst through would not allow it.

"I'm glad you're getting better."

"It's good to be feelin' better. Now, take this fuckin' soup and bring me a damn cheeseburger."

For the first time in over a week, the two of them shared a good laugh together.

Chapter 27

Like any other day of the week, Thursday afternoon at the Richmond City precinct on Broad Street was in full throttle. The telephones rang off the hook while every law breaker from prostitutes to drug dealers was hauled to the back in handcuffs, and officers' booking chairs possessed bodies who either had a complaint or had broken the law. To the average person, the police station would have appeared to be a human zoo, but, to Richmond's finest, it was just another day on the job.

"May I help you?" the desk sergeant asked the approaching figure.

"Yes, I'm looking for Detective Love," he replied.

"Is this a civil or criminal matter?" the sergeant inquired.

"More like a personal one," the man clarified. He handed the desk sergeant his credentials.

"This here's expired, mister."

"Yes, I know, but, if you'll allow me to explain—"

"Explain it to Detective Love. He's right over there in that office," the desk sergeant said as he pointed. "Just knock on the door and tell 'im Sergeant Wright gave you permission."

"Thanks, Sergeant."

Moments later, Andre Randle entered Detective Love's office per his permission.

"Good afternoon, Detective, my name is Andre Randle. I am the ex-chief of police out in Norfolk."

"Pleased to meet you, Chief." Detective Love stood and extended his hand, addressing Andre Randle respectfully. "Sit," he offered.

"Thanks."

"So, what can I do for you, Chief?" Detective Love asked, sitting back down and leaning back.

"It's more like what can we do for each other," Andre Randle answered, rephrasing his question.

Detective Love raised his eyebrows and asked, "How so?"

Andre Randle scratched his head. Then, he took a deep breath and said, "Well, the other night while I was watching the news . . ."

As soon as he mentioned the news, Detective Love clenched his teeth. He knew the conversation had something to do with what had taken place at the mental hospital and the possible connection to the murder of one of the ex-patients.

"I'm sorry, Chief, but, unless you've been assigned to this case, I'm not at liberty to discuss any of the particulars. In fact, I'm actually not even on the case as you probably may already know." Detective Love could feel his blood pressure rising.

Andre Randle also caught it. He tried to smooth things over when he said, "Detective, I apologize if I've offended you. That was not my intent. Let me be clear, so you can understand what I was getting at. A few years ago, back in Norfolk on Interstate 264, a woman was gunned down after her and an accomplice, who was her child's grandfather, fled the scene of an armored car heist."

Detective Love ran through his mental Rolodex to see if he had any recollection of the incident as he listened to Andre Randle.

"Prior to that, the woman was released from federal prison after the Supreme Court overturned her conviction for a bank robbery and a slew of murders she was alleged to have committed with her deceased boyfriend. That woman's name was Teflon Jackson. Her boyfriend's name was Treacherous Freeman, who was also the father of her son."

Detective Love looked up at the ceiling as if the answer were there. The stories Andre Randle had just disclosed to him had sounded vaguely familiar. He was trying to place where he had heard the names before.

"One of the names may ring a bell to you because it is the same name of the young man in the photo they are flashing all over the television alongside your daughter's picture," Andre Randle stated.

Detective Love rummaged through some papers on his desk until he found what he was looking for. On the back of the photo was the name TREACHEROUS FREEMAN, JR. Detective Love shook his desktop mouse and woke the screen of his computer. He typed in one of the names Andre Randle had mentioned into the Google search engine. The first thing that popped up instantly refreshed his memory. The link for an article titled BONNIE & CLYDE OF THE NEW MILLENNIUM took Detective Love back to the time when he was fresh out of the academy. The reign of terror the couple had caused swept through the police forces of the entire State of Virginia. He remembered the story being a constant topic in the morning role call for cautionary purposes.

Detective Love continued to scroll down. He found the link of the story Andre Randle had told him about the mother of the kid his daughter had become a fugitive of justice with and clicked on it.

He looked at Andre Randle. Then, he looked back at the screen's monitor.

"Is that you?" Detective Love asked as he leaned in closer to view the picture in the article.

"Yes," Andre Randle replied.

"Jeez," Detective Love said. After he had read the first few lines of the article, he asked, "What the hell happened out there?" The detective was full of curiosity.

"She had a gun pointed to her son's head and was about to pull the trigger. I had to take the shot," Andre Randle stated simply. His answer left a bad taste in his mouth.

"The same son who is now wanted for questioning in a murder?"

"Exactly," Andre Randle replied.

"And the plot thickens." Detective Love shook his head.

"Do you want to go grab a cup of coffee, so I can fill you in on all the other details?" Andre Randle suggested.

"Sounds like a good idea," Detective Love said, accepting the invitation. "I've got a feeling this is going to be a long day."

Detective Love stood and grabbed his suit jacket off the back of his chair. He couldn't help but wonder where he had gone wrong as a father as he and Andre Randle exited his office.

Chapter 28

The sound of Virginia Beach's ocean waves were like music to Treacherous's and Baby's ears when they killed the engines to their bikes and pulled off their helmets. It was the first time in over a week that the two had been out of their apartment since Baby had recovered from her withdrawal. It was also the first time the two had ever been to a beach.

Treacherous had been planning to visit the Atlantic Avenue strip where the beach was located ever since he had read about it in his mother's journals. Baby had never had the urge to go by herself and didn't have anyone she ever wanted to go with. Treacherous thought a day by the water would be perfect, so he suggested they shoot out to the beach in one of the Seven Cities. He climbed off his R1.

"Come on."

He held out his hand for Baby, who was still sitting on the stolen Honda Interceptor. Treacherous took hold of Baby's hand and guided her to the beach. He stared out into the ocean. From where he stood, he could see that the sun had just about faded behind the sea, but it was showing just enough to blanket the water like a glistening coat.

"We gonna chill here," he said as he sat down in the sand.

Baby sat beside him. "Thank you." She leaned in and kissed Treacherous on the cheek. She flashed Treacherous a smile to camouflage the tears she was fighting back. As of midnight, that day was a special day for Baby, and Treacherous was making it even more special for her. It had been awhile since anyone had shown her that they cared, and Baby was more than appreciative. There was no other place she could have seen herself being and no other person she could have imagined being with at that moment. Everything felt so right to Baby.

"For what?" Treacherous asked, already having an idea.

"Just for being you and for being here with me on my birthday."

He looked at his watch and playfully remarked, "Oh, yeah! It is your birthday. How old are you now? Sixteen?"

She punched him in the arm and said, "Nigga, don't you know you're never supposed to ask a woman her age? And for your information, I'm eight-muthafuckin'-teen. Thank you."

Treacherous smiled. "I was just messing with you. I know you're a grown-ass woman."

Baby blushed and dug her bare feet into the dampened sand. "It's nice out here."

"Yeah," Treacherous replied.

"You wanna walk?" Baby asked.

"We can."

"This sand feels good on my feet."

Baby was in high spirits. She kicked the sand as they strolled up the beach. She felt so much joy alongside the water. She jumped around and smiled at Treacherous. That was the first time in a long time that Baby felt free and safe. The sounds of waves, as they crashed on to the beach, played in the background. The breeze had a slight chill that rode on it. Baby loved every minute of it all.

"You like the water?" Baby asked.

"Yeah, I guess. Come here," Treacherous said with outstretched arms.

Baby just smiled back at him. She turned around and walked closer to the water. Treacherous followed.

"Come here," he said again. This time, his tone was stern.

Baby ignored him. She turned and smiled at him again.

"I love you."

His words came out of nowhere and stopped Baby in her tracks. She slowly turned to face him. They watched each other for a moment.

"Baby, I want you by my side forever." He let his last word linger. "I know you've been through a lot, but I promise, I'll keep you safe."

Baby jumped on Treacherous and wrapped her legs around his hips. The force of her weight caught him off guard and caused both of them to fall onto the ground of the sandy beach. Baby laughed. She kissed Treacherous on the lips and smiled at him. Then, she got up and ran toward the end of the pier. Treacherous rose to his feet. The darkness prevented him from seeing more than just her silhouette as she disappeared into the night.

"Baby!" he called out to her.

Baby could see Treacherous from where she hid. She stood barefoot in the saltwater as the waves from the tide slapped against her legs.

"Baby! Stop playing! I don't do this!"

Baby turned around and rested her back on the log. She smiled at Treacherous's words. Since she had been around him, he was so serious all the time. Baby needed to laugh and have a good time. She wanted to feel good for a second or two. Her feelings were quickly interrupted.

Out of nowhere, a hand slithered around Baby's throat and broke her good mood. A dash of fear hit her. Her heart rate sped up. She hadn't seen anyone else on the beach when she and Treacherous began their walk. She wondered where Treacherous was. She wanted to scream, but she couldn't. The hand had a firm grip around Baby's throat. The attacker's thumb was cutting into her larynx, making it difficult for her to breathe. The attacker pulled her from up against the pole and forced her to turn around. Baby closed her eyes. She felt as if she were going to pass out. All of a sudden, she felt the hand being released from around her neck. That was the break she felt she needed; she immediately sprang into action.

"Baby! What the fuck?" Treacherous threw up his guard and weaved out of the line of her punches.

"Boy! What's wrong with you? Why you do that to me?" Baby swung a sharp right hook at Treacherous, missing his chin by a mere centimeter.

"Who you thought I was? An ax murderer or something?" Treacherous laughed.

"That shit wasn't funny." On the outside, Baby was mad, but, on the inside, she was glad it was him. "Why you do that shit, Treach? That shit wasn't funny at all," Baby said as she had her hands on her knees, trying to catch her breath.

"You wanted to play," Treacherous said straight-faced.

Baby punched him.

"Damn, girl."

"Not like that."

"Aw. Did I scare the tough girl?"

"Oh, that's funny? Punk ass."

"You call me a punk ass? You the one over there with your heart racing like you seen death come out of the water or some shit. Come here."

"What?" she asked with an attitude.

"You really mad?"

Baby sucked her teeth.

A moment passed with nothing but the sound of the water hitting the poles and the sand between them. Under the pier, it was almost pitch black. The only light was the tiny bit from the street lights behind them and the small amount that bounced off the water from the moon, but the lack of light hadn't stopped Baby from spotting Treacherous's open arms. Baby moved in close, and Treacherous wrapped his arms around her. He seized her in his grasp tightly and kissed her on the neck.

When Baby glanced up at him, he squeezed her even tighter. His light brown eyes had transformed into a deeper brown. They had Baby mesmerized. The sound of his heart beat pounded in Baby's ear as she laid her head on his chest. She melted in Treacherous's embrace. His chest felt relaxing to Baby. She loved the feel of his chest muscles pressed against her face. Treacherous cupped his hand under Baby's chin and lifted her head. He kissed her passionately. Baby welcomed his full lips as he parted hers with his tongue. They stood in the water, kissing and fondling each other for what seemed like hours but, in reality, were only mere seconds.

Treacherous took Baby by the hand and guided her out of the water and onto the sand. He laid Baby on a dry portion of the beach and took off his knapsack. He bent down and kissed her again. This time, it was a slow, deep kiss. His natural body scent intoxicated Baby and ignited a flame inside of her that she never knew existed. Treacherous undressed Baby until there was nothing left. When she was completely nude, he stood up and took a step back. He admired her beauty. He had watched and studied her curves many times, but to see her smooth caramel piece of art in the flesh was indescribable to Treacherous. He loved the way her wavy hair lay across her breast.

She watched Treacherous with passion in her eyes as he took off his shirt. She had seen him without clothes many times; but that night it seemed as if she were seeing his body for the first time. She inhaled and let out a deep sigh. Her heart skipped a beat as Treacherous's chocolate skin glowed in the dark, matching his glistening, shaved head. Baby could see his print rising in his sweatpants as he loosened the drawstrings. She felt her inner thighs moisten. She spread her legs wide enough for his frame and invited Treacherous in.

Treacherous smiled. Baby's cleanly shaved pussy added to the stiffness he already possessed in his dick. He slid his sweatpants down to the ground and stepped out of them. Then, he did the same with his boxer briefs. His rock hard dick stood at attention as the cool, summer breeze, combined with the mist of the ocean, tickled his back from top to bottom. He instantly became conscious of his nudity. Treacherous looked around. No one was in sight. He moved in closer to Baby and kneeled back down. He began planting kissing on every inch of her body. Baby giggled like a little schoolgirl as he kissed around the outer lips of her vagina. Then, he concentrated on kissing her outer lips. She could feel his goatee brushing up against her skin. She enjoyed the ticklish feeling.

Baby moaned loudly and arched her back. She grabbed a fistful of sand in anticipation. No words passed between the two of them. Their eye contact and the kisses they exchanged cemented their bond.

Treacherous was inexperienced when it came to sex, but he followed his instinct. Everything felt natural to him.

Baby reached out for Treacherous and guided his dick inside her pussy. She felt a little pain as he penetrated her, but she was ready to feel him inside of her. She had experimented with sex before, but those early encounters could not compare to what she felt at that moment. Having Treacherous inside of her made her feel like a virgin. She knew they should have been using protection but she wanted to feel his flesh inside of her. Her tunnel was tight and saturated. The wetness somewhat eased the pain and assisted Treacherous through her sexual path. His length engulfed her entirely.

"Mmm," Baby cooed. "I love you," she whispered into the air. "I love—"

Treacherous's thrust cut her statement short. The feeling was all new to Treacherous. He was in pure ecstasy. It was as if he was one with Baby. Every stroke had him ready to burst, but he held firm. Treacherous cupped Baby's ass cheeks in the palms of his hands. He raised her from the sand and held her in midair as he dug deeper into her soul.

"Damn," he said out loud. "Shit, Baby."

"Yes. Ooh," she cried out.

Treacherous gazed into Baby's eyes, which were barely opened. He wanted to make sure he pleased her. He got his answer from her facial expressions as Baby tossed her head back and opened her mouth.

"Yes," she moaned. Then, she bit down on her bottom lip.

Treacherous plunged deeper. He stroked left then right.

"Oh, my God. I'm . . . Oh, shit. Treach, I'm about to come," Baby cried out.

Treacherous's pace quickened. He stirred inside of her warmth like a spoon in hot tea. Baby's entire body shuddered.

Treacherous tried to hold his own explosion, but Baby's cave was too wet for him. As her walls caved in and collapsed around his sex pole, Treacherous couldn't hold back any longer. Together, Treacherous and Baby climbed new heights. Treacherous filled her up with his juices, while she covered his dick with her cream.

Treacherous rolled over onto the sand. Baby followed him and placed her head on his chest. They both stared up at the stars.

"I really love you," Treacherous said as he ran his fingers up and down Baby's spine.

"You better," Baby replied with a smile plastered all over her face.

Baby was on cloud nine. Everything seemed flawless on the Virginia beach. She closed her eyes, and, for the first time in a long time, she felt protected.

"I bought something for you," Treacherous said to Baby.

"Treach, you didn't have to, but that's so sweet." Baby was touched that he had thought to get her a gift for her birthday.

Treacherous reached into his knapsack and pulled out a small box. "Open it up," he said, handing Baby the gift.

"Nigga, you tryin'a make me cry out here?" Baby said as she took the gift. "This is beautiful," Baby exclaimed. The thin platinum necklace with a petite motorcycle pendant nearly brought tears to Baby's eyes.

Treacherous was grinning from ear to ear. Then, he said, "Read the back."

"'To my ride or die chick: 'til death do us part,'" Baby said, reading the engraving out loud. "Thank you, babe. This is the best birthday a girl could ever ask for. I love you, Mr. Freeman."

Baby wrapped her arms around Treacherous's neck and kissed him.

"I love you too, Mrs. Freeman." Treacherous smiled.

"Don't say something you don't mean," Baby advised him.

"I won't." Treacherous reached back into his knapsack and pulled out what he had remaining in the bag and said, "I wanna share something with you."

Baby recognized the notepads.

"These pages are my life. This is all I have left of my family. Everything I know about my parents I learned in here. I never felt any connection to anything or anyone else except these notepads and my mother the day she was killed, up until now. Baby, believe me when I tell you you're all I got and, for real, all I really want and need. I wanted to share some of this with you tonight, and eventually, all of it, to let you into my world because you're a part of my family now, and I want you to know what I come from." Treacherous kissed Baby on the forehead and cracked open one of his mother's journals.

For the next thirty minutes, Baby listened attentively as Treacherous read the scene of his parents' last days together. Once he was finished reading, Treacherous folded the page where he stopped and closed the notepad.

"I chose to read that because you remind me so much of my mother," he told her. "I wanted you to hear how she rode for my father. The first time I ever read both of these notepads I couldn't wait to get older to find my ride or die chick. And now that I have, I believe I can do anything I put my mind to," Treacherous said proudly.

He was so caught up in the moment that he hadn't noticed that Baby was crying.

"Babe, don't cry. We good. Me and you against the world, right?" Treacherous wiped her tears.

"Yeah, me and you against the world, babe," Baby repeated. She wiped away the rest of her tears.

Baby positioned herself in the curve of Treacherous's armpit.

"Damn, I wish my mom was still alive to meet you," Treacherous said, wrapping his arms around Baby.

He could feel Baby's body jerking.

"Babe, what's up?" Treacherous kissed her on the top of the head. "What's wrong?" He wanted to know.

"You got me crying and shit." Baby looked up into his eyes and tried to sound hard.

"Fuck that," Treacherous retorted. "It's not about that. What's wrong with my baby?" His words were stern yet compassionate. Baby lowered her gaze and smiled. She took a deep breath. She didn't know where to begin, but she knew the timing was right.

"Since you shared something personal with me, I want to do the same to let you know that I feel the same way about you," she said.

"You don't have to if you're not ready. I already know that," Treacherous assured her.

"I know, but I want to."

"So, talk to me then. Why you keep crying and shit?"

At that moment, she felt she could tell Treacherous anything.

"You know, it's crazy," she started, "how something that happened so long ago can seem like a movie I just watched yesterday. I can still hear the water running. In my dreams, I can see the large Jacuzzi tub with the glass backdrop filled with water. The bubbles had almost flowed over the rim. I can even smell the honey from the moisturizer that was always added." Baby visualized the scene as she spoke. "It's like watching me outside of myself." She shook her head and wiped her eyes in an attempt to fight off the tears that were now flowing heavily.

"Baby, what are you talking about?" Treacherous wanted to know.

"I remember the water being hot, almost too hot," Baby continued as she transported Treacherous into her nightmare. She closed her eyes and was no longer nestled up under him. She was back where it had all began.

Jaz stood to the side, watching as Baby bathed. After a few minutes, she made her way over to the tub. She took the washcloth out of Baby's hand and bathed her. She made her way down Baby's back and into the water.

"Stand up," she told her. Baby did as she was told.

Baby rose out of the water slowly.

"Turn around," Jaz instructed her.

Baby turned to face her. Jaz rubbed the washcloth across Baby's chest and stomach. Baby chuckled from Jaz's touch. Jaz smiled at her and said, "You like that, baby girl?"

"Yes. It tickles," Baby's little voice said.

She rubbed the front of Baby's legs with the soapy washcloth. Then, she slid her way in between them. Jaz used the washcloth to clean Baby's vagina. As she did, Baby sang one of her favorite songs.

"'It's just one of dem days, when I wanna be all alone.'" Baby sang the lyrics to Monica's song while Jaz continued to wash between her legs. "'It's just one of dem days. Don't take it personal.'"

"You know I love it when you sing. Your voice is so pretty," Jaz told her.

"Thank you." Baby blushed.

"Open your legs some more for me," Jaz instructed, while she matched Baby's smile.

Without a thought, Baby spread her legs wider, so Jaz could clean her everywhere.

"'It's just one of dem days, and you think I treat you wrong.'"

The water felt good on her skin, and the singing made Baby feel joy inside. She had always relished her baths.

Jaz's smile gave Baby comfort. Jaz continued to smile at Baby as she replaced the washcloth with her finger. Jaz used it to fondle and caress Baby's young clit. Baby didn't understand what was going on. She stood there frozen as she watched Jaz close her eyes a couple of times. Baby's body started to experience a peculiar sensation as Jaz rubbed her hand in circular motions between her legs.

"Baby, you like that?" Jaz asked as if she had been giving Baby some type of gift or surprise. Baby shrugged her shoulders.

"Don't worry. You will. Stay still and keep singing that pretty song. I'm going to give you something else, okay?" Jaz maintained her smile.

Baby nodded her head and did as she was told.

"'It's one of dem days,'" Baby continued singing. The more Jaz caressed Baby's flesh, the more Baby felt what seemed like a prickling up her spine. Then, an uncontrollable feeling flowed through Baby's body. Baby liked the feeling and laughed.

"Sit back down," Jaz said smiling at Baby.

Jaz leaned over and into the tub. She continued to wash every inch of Baby's body. Together, they sang Baby's favorite song.

"That was fun," Baby said delighted at her new bath game.

"You know I love you, right?" Jaz asked Baby, wrapping a towel around her body as she lifted her out of the water.

"Yes," Baby said as she threw her arms around Jaz's neck.

"We're a team, right?" Jaz asked.

"Yes."

"A team with our own secret games," Jaz added.

Baby didn't quite understand what Jaz meant by "secret games," but she loved Jaz, and, if the game they had just played was supposed be a secret one, then she wouldn't tell a soul.

"You know what? Let's get you dressed and go get you a new dress. How does that sound?" Jaz said, helping Baby out of the bathtub.

"Yay!" Baby cheered with excitement.

Jaz gave Baby a smile as they headed for the bedroom. Once they were there, she spread lotion all over Baby's body. As she did, there was a knock on the door.

"One minute," she yelled.

"Jaz, it's me. I wanna see my niece."

"You can't come in, Uncle Gary. I'm getting dressed." Baby smiled at the sound of her uncle's voice.

"Okay, baby girl. I'll see you when you get downstairs."

"Okay," Baby yelled back as she smiled.

Once she was completely dressed and her hair had been pulled back into a ponytail, Jaz and Baby headed down the stairs, parting ways at the bottom of the staircase. The house was buzzing with the entire clan. It was the day before Thanksgiving and two days before Baby's eleventh birthday.

As Baby entered the living room, she spotted her father. The sight of him made her smile inside and out. Baby adored her father more than anyone else in the world. To her, he was a hero. He was standing to the left of her favorite window. She ran over to him and bolted into his arms.

"Baby, you're gonna have to stop jumping on me like that. You are getting too big for me to be catching you. Don't you think?"

"Does that mean I'm not your baby girl anymore?" Baby smiled at her father.

"You'll always be my baby girl," he said, hugging Baby again.

"Why didn't you tell him?"

Baby's emotional scene came to a halt at the sound of Treacherous's voice.

"Tell him what?" Baby replied, returning to the present. She rose up.

"What happened?"

"What do you mean? Didn't you hear me? I didn't know my damn self." Baby was angry now. "I was only ten. How the fuck was I supposed to know what she was doing?"

"My fault, babe. You're right. You couldn't have known," Treacherous consoled her. He felt stupid for saying what he had said. The last thing he wanted to do was ruin what he believed to be one of the best days of his life.

"That shit is a thing of the past," he added. "Nobody's never gonna hurt you ever again, not while I'm livin'!" Treacherous boldly stated. "'Til death do us part."

"'Til death do us part," Baby repeated.

Baby lay back down on Treacherous and stared up into his eyes. "I didn't mean to snap on you like that. It's just—"

"You didn't do anything wrong. I wasn't thinking," Treacherous cut her off. "Forget about all of that for now, though. Let's not worry about all the fucked-up shit that we done been through," Treacherous told her. "We need to focus on getting some money, so we can survive 'cause we're just about out. Trust me. After that, we can deal with all the other shit."

Treacherous looked down at her to make sure she had heard him.

Baby shook her head in agreement. "I know a way we can get some quick money," she said.

"How?"

Baby smiled and began to share her idea with Treacherous, who was all ears.

Chapter 29

Jazmyne Love had spent the last two hours in the kitchen preparing one of her signature meals. First, she had separated the corn from the cob. Then, she fried the corn with onions. The seasoned red potatoes were boiling. They would be made into mashed potatoes. She had let the meat marinate before putting it in the oven to bake. She set the table for two. Then, she dimmed the lights and pulled out one of her favorite CDs to set the mood.

"How was your day, honey?" Jazmyne asked her husband who had just arrived home.

"It was okay. What did you cook?" he asked, wanting to change the subject.

He patiently waited for his wife to place his meal in front of him. He was deep in thought and knew that she would pick up on it. He was not in the mood to talk, though. He just wanted to eat and go to bed. Arthur Love tried to conceal his day from his wife knowing it would just cause tension, but his body language gave him away.

As Jazmyne prepared her husband's plate, she couldn't help but notice the disturbed look written all over his face. She hoped it wasn't anything that would kill the evening she intended to enjoy with him.

"Barbequed turkey wings," Jazmyne replied, coming out of the kitchen with a hot, steamy plate. She set the plate in front of him.

"Thank you," Arthur Love said before he bowed his head and said grace.

Jazmyne observed her husband from where she sat as he devoured his food and glass of Pepsi within a matter of minutes.

"Honey, you okay?" Jazmyne studied her husband.

Arthur Love just nodded his head. Jazmyne had been with her husband long enough to know all of his emotional sides. Complete silence only meant one of two things: he was either annoyed by something or someone, or he was simply exhausted.

Jazmyne rose from her seat and strolled over to her husband. She took his face in her hands and kissed his lips. She could almost feel the stress in his exchange. She opened her eyes to find his deep brown ones staring back at her. She tried to kiss him again, but he pulled away.

"Art, honey, what's wrong?" Jazmyne was becoming agitated.

Arthur Love rolled his eyes at his wife. Then, he got up and took his plate and glass into the kitchen. The sight of him sidestepping past her and leaving her hanging made the hairs stand up on Jazmyne's arms. She spun around and followed behind him. When she entered the kitchen, she spotted him posted up on the counter. The look on his face caused her anger to subside.

"You had a bad day?"

He turned to her. Jazmyne stepped in front of him. She stood on her tippy toes in order to kiss him directly on the forehead. He returned the gesture with crossed arms and a deep breath. Jazmyne dismissed his reaction. Instead, she ran her hand across his face and kissed his left cheek. In the background, Glenn Lewis's "It's Not Fair" bellowed in the air. She gave him tiny kisses on his lips and his neck. Simultaneously, her left hand traveled down the center of his chest while her right hand headed for his belt buckle. Jazmyne closed her eyes, bent her knees, and followed her hands. She had thought that if she could take her husband's mental to another place, for even a moment, it might help things.

"Are you serious? Tsk," he said and jerked her hand from his waist and walked away.

"What the fuck?" she shrieked, following him. "What the hell is your problem? It better not be what I think it is."

Arthur Love headed up the stairs. He wasn't in the mood to fight or to have sex.

"Art! I'm talking to you! Come here!" She was pissed, and she didn't want to leave it alone. She knew that it had something to do with Baby, and it had her on fire.

As Arthur Love disappeared into the bedroom, Jazmyne followed him.

"I don't want to talk. I already know what you're going to say. I've heard it all before," he stated.

"You don't want to talk. You leave me downstairs on my fucking knees, and you don't want to talk?"

Jazmyne was fuming. She rarely used profanity toward her husband. For the most part, she never even raised her voice at him. He would have had to bring her to a breaking point for her to even think about speaking to him in such a manner. In all the years they'd been together, they had rarely had big fights. However, during the few altercation that they did have, it was Jazmyne who always held her tongue and tried to keep the peace; but the few times that she was unable to always caught Art off guard, and this time was no different.

Arthur Love turned to his wife. "Who are you talking to like that?"

"You! Really? Are we going to start this shit again?" she said and moved in to close the gap between them. "I thought we had agreed that you weren't going to bring your work home. You promised me that you'd leave that shit at the door, no matter what it was."

Arthur Love attempted to leave the room.

"No. You're not going anywhere until you either tell me what's wrong or you put a fucking smile on your face."

"Jazmyne, you better move," he said, stepping to the side again.

Jazmyne stood firm with her hands on her hips. Arthur Love shook his head. Then, he scooped her off her feet, threw her over his shoulder, and slammed her roughly onto the bed. The impact of her body hitting the king-sized bed nearly knocked the wind out of her.

"I told you to get the hell out of my way," were his final words before he walked away from the bed. Arthur Love stormed out of his bedroom, leaving Jazmyne Love gasping for air and staring up at the ceiling.

Chapter 30

As usual, Treacherous couldn't help but admire the three customized, chromed-out bikes that were lined up on the lawn of the Glen Allen home. For weeks, he had been seeing the beautiful machines and couldn't wait until he made one of them his own. Although all of them were equally a work of art in his eyes, from the Hayabusa down to the BMW S1000RR, the Yamaha R1 stood out to Treacherous above all.

"See you later, girl," he whispered as he maneuvered his way to the front door, stealth-like. He admired how the chrome engine and dual pipes complemented the bike. He became aroused at the site and made a mental note to himself to return to it after he finished taking care of business.

As he reached the door, Treacherous pulled out his black .40-caliber and cocked it. The brisk fall air felt good to him and seemed to heighten all of his senses. Regardless of the fact that he was a solid 225 pounds and an even six feet tall, the black hoodie sweat suit and Timberlands he wore made him nearly invisible, blending in with the darkness.

He pulled the black mask he was formerly wearing on top of his head down over his face, then flipped the hood of his sweatshirt over top of it and drew in the strings, until only his eyes and mouth could be seen.

Treacherous could hear the loud music thumping in the house, but he couldn't decide which one was louder, his heartbeat or the bass line. He had the usual butterflies in his stomach. No matter how many robberies he pulled off, they would always show up and float around in his belly. He thought about his parents, wondering how they had felt when they were in similar situations.

Treacherous slowly opened the screen door and put the key inside the lock. He gently twisted it back and forth, but to no avail. Treacherous cursed, realizing that he might have had to force himself into the house, which was not a part of his plan. He was sure that the key, because it was brand new, had something to do with it. Despite his immediate frustration, Treacherous continued to jiggle the key gently inside the lock, but he received the same results. He looked up in the air as he always did when something seemed to be going wrong. That was when he saw that familiar face smiling down at him. Treacherous focused back on the key and closed his eyes.

"Come on, baby," he whispered, right before trying the key again.

Finally, he felt the lock turning. *Let's get this money,* was his final thought as he eased the door open and slid inside.

As soon as he entered the house, he spotted a young kid nearly his age rolling up a blunt. He had his back turned to Treacherous and was oblivious to the imminent danger that was creeping up on him. The loud music had drowned out any noise that Treacherous might have made, but the sudden gust of cold air that followed him inside had hit the back of the kid's neck and alarmed him, making him aware of Treacherous's presence.

His eyes widened in shock and fear when he saw Treacherous, who quickly closed the distance between them. Wasting no time, Treacherous viciously brought the gun down on the hustler's head. The butt of the hammer crashed into the kid's forehead, instantly knocking him out. He hit the ground with a thud. Treacherous prayed that nobody else had heard it.

He quickly dug into the young boy's pockets until he found what he was looking for: a nice thick wad of money. He then relieved him of the jewelry he wore around his neck and wrist along with the kid's gun tucked in his belt and tossed them in a drawstring bag. Treacherous was thankful of the loud music despite it being nerve-racking. As gangsta as he was, he despised gangsta rap. He believed that gangsta rappers profited off of a type of lifestyle they really knew nothing about and one he felt he was forced to live. He had a problem with the fact that, while gangsta rappers received millions of dollars for rapping about "thug life" and "ballin," the people who really lived it received millions of years in prison or a life sentence in the cemetery.

As he crept down the hallway, he could hear the music blaring through the surround sound. Treacherous silently eased himself next to the bedroom. He could hear several voices in there and was in the process of trying to figure out exactly how many people were in the room when a voice yelled, "Where the fuck Red at wit' dat blunt? Li'l greasy-ass muthafucka probably trying to take it to the head."

Treacherous heard footsteps approaching. He quickly slipped into the room, surprising a heavyset, dark-skinned man with cornrows who was about to walk out. Before anybody could react, Treacherous savagely swung his pistol and delivered a riveting blow to the heavyset man's face, while also shoving him backward. The man scrambled to get up, but his brain moved in slow motion. It hadn't registered in his mind yet what had just happened to him. The weed and liquor had him stuck.

The combination of the blood that was now pouring out of the gash the gun had created on his upper lip and the pain that had set in caused him to collapse on his back.

His dazed, intoxicated eyes stared up at Treacherous. There was complete silence in the room until Treacherous calmly spoke, saying, "All I want is the money."

He did a quick head count. Not including the young kid at the door, there was a total of six people: three men and three women.

Two women—one caramel toned, and the other with a high-yellow complexion—sat there in boy shorts and wife beaters. Both had large breasts. Right next to them was a medium-build, brown-skinned man with shoulder-length dreadlocks. On the other side of him was a dark chocolate beauty wearing only a thong and a baby tee. Her chest was big, but it was not as big as the other two chicks'. She, however, made up for it with her lower half. Her thighs were thick and solid. *She is built like a stallion,* thought Treacherous.

Treacherous's eyes came to rest on the one known as Dre, a coal black slim brother with a low brush cut. He wore a wife beater and baggy jeans. He clutched a half gallon of Grey Goose in one hand and the TV remote in the other. *Unlike everybody else in this room, there is no fear in dude's eyes,* thought Treacherous. He knew that could be a problem, one that he was prepared to handle if need be.

The wounded man on the floor moaned in pain.

"You a'ight, Bo?" Dre asked, never taking his eyes off Treacherous.

"Nah, man. I think this nigga broke my shit," Bo mumbled, spitting a glob of blood on the floor.

"Fuck all dat," Treacherous said, matching Dre's stare with one that confirmed he meant business. "Where the paper at?"

Dre ignored his question and asked one of his own. "How the fuck you get in here?"

"Ya boy Red lemme in."

Treacherous's answer got a reaction out of Dre. He narrowed his eyes and clenched his jaw. "That li'l faggot mu'fucka set—"

"He dead now," Treacherous calmly stated, cutting Dre off.

That comment struck home as Dre's mouth hung open in disbelief, while Bo, forgetting about his own pains, pounded his fists into the floor. Both chicks gasped, covering their mouths. The brown-skinned dread's face never changed, but he balled his hands up into tight fists, and the chocolate beauty sat there, wide-eyed, but she did not know what to say or do. Each person in the room had love for Red. They were a team, and, up until his demise, he was a part of it. The heavy, pungent aroma of marijuana hung heavily in the room while the sounds of hip-hop continued to blare through the speakers.

Treacherous felt like the rapper was personally talking to him. He decided to take things into his own hands.

"You," he barked, pointing the gun at the caramel chick. "Get cha ass over here."

She slowly got off the sofa and walked toward Treacherous, who pulled out the drawstring bag and handed it to her.

"I want you to walk around to each one of these niggas and run their pockets. I want their money, jewels, drugs, cell phones, and guns. I want everything. You understand me? Put it all in this bag. If you try anything stupid, I'ma shoot you in ya fuckin' face, a'ight?"

She dumbly nodded her head.

"Starting with you. Put all ya jewelry in the bag," Treacherous ordered.

"Not my bracelet. My mother gave me this," she protested.

"Bitch!" Treacherous snapped. He backhanded the girl. It sounded like a firecracker had exploded. He roughly grabbed the back of her head by her hair, while keeping his eyes glued on Dre and the others.

Then, he said menacingly, "Put every muthafuckin' thing in the bag, you hear me?"

Afterward, she complied with his order, removing all of her jewelry and placing it in the bag. She then walked over to Bo and repeated the process with him.

"C'mere, light skin," Treacherous ordered.

Unafraid, she headed over to him. She was actually turned on by his presence. She knew the big man in front of her meant business, and she was attracted to that. All her life she had dealt with thorough street guys in Virginia, so she could spot one a mile away. He had killed Red, pistol whipped Bo, smacked the fire out of her peoples Ke-Ke, and, if he was crazy enough to rob her boo Dre, then, in her book, that meant he was as thorough as they came, or he just didn't have it all.

For the average man, the girl's body would have been a distraction, but not for Treacherous. He paid her physical no mind because he was focused on one thing. As she approached him, Treacherous could see that her nipples were erect. They looked as if they would poke through the fabric at any minute.

"Listen. I want you to follow her and strip all these chump asses naked. Can you handle that, sweetheart?" Treacherous spoke in a gentle voice.

She nodded her head and whispered, "Yes."

"Good," Treacherous stated. He noticed the seductive look in the girl's eyes and decided to use it to his advantage. "Thanks, sexy," he said as a half smile formed through the mask.

Despite the situation, the light-skinned girl, whose name was Shay, found herself extremely horny. Maybe it was the fact that Treacherous was a dangerous man in the middle of doing dangerous things but he still took time out to compliment her. That was something Dre hadn't done in quite some time. Whatever it was, Shay's pussy was soaking wet, and she prayed that everybody lived through this, so maybe she, Dre, and her homegirl could engage in a threesome. The thought put a smile on her face.

Dre saw this and wondered why his chick was smiling. *That bitch set me the fuck up. She in on this shit,* he thought.

Shay followed Ke-Ke, stripping Bo naked, then Dre, and finally the dread. Within minutes, Treacherous was the only man in the room who was fully clothed. Ke-Ke handed the bag back to Treacherous loaded with money jewelry and weapons.

"A'ight, you got the shit. Now, get the fuck outta here!" Dre snapped. Despite being completely naked and caught slipping, he attempted to maintain his boss status.

"Nah, I said I wanted all of it. Everything! This ain't everything, mu'fucka. Where's the rest of it at?" Treacherous asked, aiming the gun at Dre who calmly took a sip from the Grey Goose bottle, ignoring the question.

Treacherous snorted. "Oh, you wanna act stupid, nigga? Well, let's act stupid then."

He roughly snatched up the kid with the dreads and forced him to his knees. He, then, rammed the muzzle of the .40-caliber through the mass of hair until it hit skull.

"What's your name, chump?" Treacherous asked the kid, keeping his eyes on Dre the entire time.

"K . . . Kyle," the dude stammered, scared to death.

"Well, Kyle, you in a fucked-up situation right about now 'cause ya man over there trying to hold out on me. Now, I'ma count to three, and if he don't gimme the rest of the money, it's gonna be ugly for you, my dude," Treacherous informed him before he began his count.

Kyle nervously looked over at Dre, who was unfazed by the scene.

"One," Treacherous began.

"Yo! Give him the fuckin' money, Dre," Bo pleaded through his busted, bloody lips.

"Shut the fuck up!" Dre barked, never taking his eyes off of Treacherous.

"You don't give a fuck. I don't give a fuck. This ya manz, not mines," Treacherous spewed.

Dre said nothing.

Treacherous shrugged his shoulders. "Two," he called out.

"What the fuck is wrong wit' you?" Kyle cried out in fear. "Pay him! Give him the fuckin' money, Dre!"

Dre snickered and took another swig of the Grey Goose.

"I suggest you listen to this man," Treacherous advised, but Dre remained glued to his seat, refusing to back down. Treacherous pressed the gun even harder into Kyle's skull.

"Thr—"

"Okay! Okay! I'll give you the money! Please don't shoot him! Please," Shay screamed out. She had seen enough. Although she had seen people killed before, this was different. Kyle was her cousin, and she knew she would not be able to live with herself or face her favorite aunt if she had witnessed her cousin's murder. She was convinced that Dre was going to let her cousin get killed over some money that was replaceable. She was glad she had paid attention when Dre handled his money in front of her.

"Bitch! You down with this nigga," Dre spat, stating it rather than asking.

"No, nigga. I'm down with my cousin, who you was just about to let get killed over some fuckin' money," she spit back.

"Go get the money, sweetheart," Treacherous said, interrupting Dre and Shay's conversation.

Dre shot Shay a murderous ice grill that made her hesitate, but only for a second. She got up and made her way over to the closet. Within seconds, she was headed toward Treacherous with a Timberland box in her hands.

"Open it up for me, sexy," Treacherous instructed.

The stacks of money and the brick of coke triggered a huge smile on Treacherous's face. *Unbelievable, cheap-ass mu'fucka don't even have his shit in a safe,* thought Treacherous. After making her dump all of it in the bag, Treacherous roughly shoved Shay onto the couch and placed the gun back on Kyle's head.

"That's ya mans an' 'em," Treacherous slyly remarked.

"What are you doing? He gave you the money," Shay gasped.

"No, he didn't. He ain't give me shit! You gave me the money. I see I gotta teach his tough ass a lesson 'cause he ain't learned shit from this."

All eyes were on Treacherous now, waiting to see what he would do next. They didn't have long to wait.

Treacherous raised the gun, aimed, and squeezed. The first slug erupted out of the gun and struck the Grey Goose bottle that Dre was holding. It exploded upon impact, sending liquor and glass everywhere. Treacherous, then, sent a slug through the enormous flat-screen television, showering everybody with bits of glass. The shots were thunderous in the small room, drowning out the shouts and screams.

Treacherous waved the gun around, making sure everybody got a chance to see the big, black hole that spit death. This caused panic and chaos in the room. The shots caused Dre to sober up. Where he was once so tough, he was now terrified. Instinctively, as a means of survival, he pulled Shay on top of him, using her as a shield. She screamed and protested, but Dre was too strong for her. Bo was curled up in the fetal position, whimpering and crying like a child. No one knew whether Treacherous was shooting to kill and was just a bad shot or intended to hit what he had. Either way, no one was willing to stand in the line of fire to find out.

The caramel chick dove into the closet. Treacherous lowered the gun back on Kyle.

"Who owns the green bike outside?" he asked Kyle.

"That's Dre's," he quickly replied.

"I figured dat." Treacherous chuckled. "Where the keys at?"

Dre protested, "Nah, fuck dat! You ain't takin'—"

The shot that whizzed past his head was enough to silence him.

"I'm not talkin' to you, nigga. I'm talkin' to Kyle. Say another muthafuckin' word and the next one's gonna be between your eyes!"

"The keys are all hangin' by the door," Kyle blurted out.

"Thanks, my man."

Then, all in one motion, Treacherous kicked Kyle forward and fired at the same time. Screams and yells could be heard as Treacherous backed out of the room and began jogging down the hall. He glanced at his watch. It read 1:46 a.m.

"Shit," Treacherous cursed to himself. The robbery had taken entirely too long. He was about to walk out of the house, when he spotted the motionless boy lying on the floor. Treacherous walked over to him and placed the spare key in his hand. Then, he snatched up every set of keys that were hanging where Kyle had told him. Once all the keys were in his hand, he hit the door and slipped outside, into the cool night air.

Rather than making his way around the corner where he had parked the stolen motorcycle, Treacherous immediately located the key that belonged to the R1 and hopped on it. He knew at that point Dre and his crew were up and scrambling around the room, trying to get dressed. He figured they had probably just realized he hadn't shot Kyle but rather shot the floor in between Kyle's knees, giving the impression that he had shot him in the back. As Treacherous fired up the bike, he thought about the award-winning performance he had seen in there. His partner was something else. They both deserved Oscars for their acting.

Treacherous made the Yamaha roar as he pulled off with rapid speed. Two blocks away, he imagined the look on Dre's face when he discovered Red wasn't dead and found the spare key he possessed in his hand.

Chapter 31

Andre Randle took another swig of his beer as he studied one of the files he had been fortunate enough to obtain. Thanks to a favor owed to him at his old precinct, he was able to get the entire criminal history on the parents of young Treacherous, as well as the father of Treacherous Sr. He had actually known the history of Teflon Jackson like he knew the back of his hand, but he wanted to know more about the males she had so willingly put her life and freedom on the line for.

During his research, he discovered that her father was her mother's pimp and that the two had killed one another. Thereafter, she resorted to a life of petty crime before hooking up with a known drug dealer who manipulated her into taking the rap for him. This landed her in the Norfolk Detention Center. He knew it was in there that she had met her son's father and joined him in a reign of terror throughout the Seven Cities, and God only knows where else they traveled. He also knew that the motive for her and her son's grandfather hitting the armored car was to gain funds, so they could kidnap her son and disappear, but, thanks to him, that plan never got a chance to be carried out totally.

Andre Randle shook his head as he read the rap sheets of both Richard "Richie Gunz" Robinson and Treacherous Freeman Sr. Ironically, both men's records were similar. The only things Richard Robinson really had on his jacket had been as a juvenile. He had shot another kid and served a year in the youth house. Then, there was the bank he had been convicted of robbing as an adult. Prior to that, there was no real criminal history on him. Treacherous Freeman Sr.'s jacket consisted of weapons possession as a juvenile and, then, ultimately, as an adult, the robbing of the same bank his father had been convicted of robbing. Only, this time, murder was added to his short criminal record. As he studied the pattern of the two men, he couldn't help but wonder if Treacherous Jr. intended to rob a bank himself.

Andre Randle picked up a pen and jotted down the thought on a notepad with the rest of the notes he had written down. He finished the remainder of his beer. Then, he gathered all of the papers that were in disarray on the coffee table.

"You can run, but you can't hide forever, kid," Andre Randle said aloud to himself.

He, then, stood and made his way to the refrigerator. He grabbed another beer and popped the top. After chugging the beer down in just five gulps, he snatched up his car keys and headed out the door to his favorite bar.

Chapter 32

Treacherous woke to the sound of a hammer being cocked. When he opened his eyes, he was not surprised to see who the intruder was. Even though he hadn't expected to see them so soon, he wondered how long it would be before they arrived. He remained still and stared down the barrel, which was pointed at his face.

"Nigga, I should blow your fuckin' head off," the intruder chimed.

"I don't blame you. If I were you, I would shoot me too," Treacherous replied.

"I don't wanna hear that shit," the intruder spat. "Matter of fact, let me see your hands, you slick-ass nigga," the intruder stated, grabbing a fistful of the sheet covering Treacherous's body.

The intruder was not surprised by what was seen when Treacherous's body was uncovered.

"Ain't no fun when the rabbit got the gun, huh? Oh, excuse me, guns!" Treacherous sarcastically remarked, referring to the twin .40s he had pointing at the intruder.

"Fuck you!" Baby dryly remarked, rolling her eyes.

"What's the matter with you? Did I hit you too hard back there or something?" Treacherous asked, thinking that the blow he had delivered back at Dre's house may have been a little too extreme. He had thought the idea was too much when Baby suggested it, but she had convinced him it was necessary to keep the suspicion off of her. It was the first time he had ever hit her or any woman, for that matter, and he wasn't sure if he could pull it off properly.

"No, nigga, that shit didn't faze me," she clarified. "What bothered me was the way you were talkin' to that bitch Shay!"

The surprised look on Treacherous's face told Baby he didn't get it.

"How the fuck you gonna call that bitch what you be calling me and talkin' that 'she sexy' shit! You think that bitch sexy?"

Treacherous just stood there, dumbfounded, shaking his head and smiling.

"It's not funny, Treach. You think that bitch'll be sexy if I go blow her fuckin' face off with the new shottie we just got?"

"Calm down." Treacherous reached for her.

Baby pulled away and yelled, "No! I am calm! Don't touch me! Go touch that bitch! You lucky I didn't want to mess up the plan or else I would've jumped up and started shootin' everybody up in that damn house, including you. Talkin' about 'thank you, sweetheart.'"

After she finished her rant, Treacherous was grinning from ear to ear behind Baby's jealousy. "Babe, come here," he said, reaching for her for the second time. Again, she pulled away.

"Man, come here!" This time, he leaned in and grabbed her forcefully and embraced her. She tried to protest, but his hug had melted her. There was no other place she felt safer than in his arms. Treacherous kissed her on top of her head.

"Babe, you buggin'. You know you the only one for me. I love you, girl. You my rider and you're crazy if you don't know that," Treacherous said, trying to reassure Baby.

She looked up and stared Treacherous in the eyes. "I'm not buggin'. I love you too, but that was some disrespectful shit, talkin' to her like that in front of me. Playing or not, job or not, I didn't like it. You lucky you didn't call her babe 'cause I would've fuckin' lost it up in that bitch."

Treacherous squeezed her tighter. "I apologize for making you feel like that. You know I'd never do anything to intentionally hurt you. You all I got, babe. And all I want, too."

He lowered his head and kissed her on the lips. The first two kisses were short, but the third was deep. He parted her lips with his tongue and probed her mouth. Baby embraced the kiss and wrapped her arms around his neck while standing on her tippy toes. Treacherous lowered his monstrous hands and cupped her ass. His kiss became more passionate as he palmed her cheeks.

While still in a lip lock, he scrunched down and lifted Baby up. She wrapped her legs around his waist as she massaged his clean-shaven head as if it were a crystal ball that could see the future. Treacherous spun her around and guided her to the king-sized bed. His sex sword had already risen to attention and was ready to be tended to. After last night's rush, he couldn't wait until his partner in crime made her way back home to him.

Baby felt Treacherous's dick brush up against her sex as he laid her on the bed. The brief encounter caused her clit to jump, adding moisture to her already throbbing pussy. She stared at him with lustful eyes. She undressed herself on the bed, while Treacherous relieved himself of his wife beater and boxer briefs, revealing his well-sculpted, almond-colored chest, shadowed six pack, and every inch of his length. She licked her lips as he moved in closer. Before he could make the next move, Baby had taken him into her mouth. Treacherous tossed his head back and placed his hands on the sides of Baby's face as he moaned in ecstasy. Baby cupped his sack with her left hand while jerking him with her right and bobbing on three inches of the eight he possessed.

The sounds of slurping, humming, moaning, and sucking filled the room, heightening Treacherous's arousal. He loved the way Baby went down on him. *It gets better each time,* he thought as he looked down at her. By now, Baby was using both hands as if she were ringing out a washcloth, while popping the head of Treacherous's hardness in and out of her mouth like her favorite lollipop.

"Fuck!" he growled as Baby stuck out her tongue and smacked it with his dick. Then, all in one motion, she took his entire manhood into her mouth. She gagged the first two times as Treacherous's helmet hit the back of her throat, but, once her tonsils relaxed, she expertly swallowed his entire eight inches in full. Treacherous clenched the bed sheets tightly while Baby displayed a phenomenal toe-curling performance. She cupped his sack as she came up off of his rock hard and ran her tongue up the length of his spine. Treacherous felt his juices building up as Baby tongue tickled his dick.

"Babe, I feel it. That shit about to—"

Before he could get the words out, Baby slipped him back into her mouth and vigorously attacked his manhood. Treacherous's body became tense as he grabbed hold of Baby's shoulder blades. Baby continued her breaststroke maneuver with her neck as she felt and tasted the warm juices of Treacherous's smoking gun spewing into her mouth. She jerked his dick with her right hand while draining the remainder of his cum from the helmet with her lips. Treacherous stared down at her with satisfied eyes.

"I fuckin' love your ass. Can't no other bitch ever replace you," he stated sincerely.

"If she did, she'd be a dead bitch! I love your punk ass too, babe."

Baby slithered up into Treacherous's embrace and closed her eyes.

Chapter 33

Detective George Parks tapped his knuckles on Detective Arthur Love's office door before letting himself in. The young detective smiled when he saw Detective Love shaking his head.

"What?" He laughed. "I knocked."

"I think you do that just to piss me off, Parks." Detective Love smirked.

"Now, why would I do that?" Detective Parks threw his hands up in the air.

In all honesty, he, along with everybody else at the precinct, knew how much Detective Love hated for someone to enter his office without permission. It was a pet peeve of his that had gotten many of their colleagues cursed out, but Detective Parks knew he was the head detective's favorite ever since he had aided him in cracking a murder case four years ago while still wet behind the ears and fresh out of the academy.

It was the small piece of evidence everyone else had overlooked that Detective Parks had discovered that got the conviction to stick. Detective Love admired how Detective Parks had doubled back to the alleged killer's mother's house and questioned her. It was the alleged killer's mother's memo pad that had actually convicted her son. Thinking she was helping her son, believing him to be innocent, she told the detective about a note he had left her the day of the murder that she had thrown away weeks prior. She was sure the note would have put her son in the clear had she still possessed it. Detective Parks asked to see the memo pad. He took a No. 2 pencil and used the side of it to shade the page. It was then Detective Parks discovered the holes needed to poke in the convicted killer's alibi. The killer had given specific times and locations of his whereabouts, but the indention of the note he had left for his mother, who had been at work while the crime was being committed, revealed the truth and conflicted his story. Detective Love found that to be genius detective work and had taken a liking to the twenty-four-year-old detective because of it.

"So, what's up? I'm sure you didn't come in here just to annoy me," Detective Love surmised.

Detective Parks's mood changed. He had almost forgotten why he had come to Detective Love's office in the first place. He took a deep breath. "I got some bad news, and I got some more bad news. Which do you want first?" Detective Parks tried to make light of the situation.

Detective Love leaned back in his chair and sighed, expecting the worst. "Whatchu got?"

"Remember the kid back at the crack house?"

"Yeah."

"Well, initially, nothing came back, but ballistics just called. They finally found a DNA match on the saliva."

Detective Love leaned in.

"Belonged to the kid Treacherous Freeman."

"Son of a bitch!" Detective Love cursed.

"Come to find out, the kid Anthony Morris was released from the same mental hospital this kid Freeman and your . . ." Detective Parks paused.

"It's okay, Parks. It is what it is." Detective Love appreciated Detective Parks's discretion.

Detective Parks moved on and continued, "Well, according to the doctor at the facility, Morris and Freeman were not too fond of one another, so we have some type of motive."

"What do you have on my daughter?" Detective Love knew he was holding back.

"Remember when Officer Bronson spotted the clear area by the door? Well, fibers matched your kid. We don't know why she was lying there, but it was definitely her." He inhaled. "They're also the same fibers that we found on the pillow used to suffocate your boy at the Super 8 over on Midlothian Turnpike."

"Goddamn it. What the hell is she . . ." Detective Love got choked up midsentence.

The news about his daughter being tied into all that had been going on in the city was a lot for him to swallow. He was known for being a big and strong man, but the situation with his only child had been weakening him slowly but surely, and now the disturbing news had broken him down like, a double-barrel shotgun.

"I'm sorry, sir," Detective Parks offered. "Just thought I should be the one to tell you before it hit the press."

"Thanks, Parks."

As Detective Parks excused himself, Arthur Love grabbed his face with both hands and wiped it. He couldn't believe this was happening. Why him? He wondered. He felt he was being punished without just cause. While so many fathers had abandoned their children, Arthur Love was the total opposite. He believed as a father he had done everything right. He had provided food, clothes, and a safe shelter for his child. He had showered her with gifts and presents when she deserved them and just because and had blanketed her with his presence as a father day in and day out.

Arthur Love closed his eyes and envisioned the last beautiful moment he'd had with his daughter on Father's Day when she was fourteen. He had looked at her and wondered where his little girl had gone. He did not want to believe that who his colleagues were accusing of the heinous crimes and his daughter were one and the same, but, the fact of the matter was that was the reality of it. With that being his conclusion, Detective Love picked up his phone.

"Hey, Randle. It's me. We need to talk."

Chapter 34

Per his request, Baby put down the television remote and slid off the bed. Then, she straddled Treacherous in her wife beater and boy shorts and rode his back while he conducted another set of pushups. Her 130 pounds added to Treacherous's now 235 pounds and increased the weight he pushed up. Baby smiled as he counted out loud. She loved watching him work out. She admired each muscle in the upper part of his back as she watched them rotate and tighten with each pushup. When he reached the number ninety-nine and came up, Baby flung her arms around his neck.

"Remember this, nigga?" Baby chimed. She applied pressure around Treacherous's throat.

Treacherous tensed up, making an attempt to break free of Baby's chokehold, but she had gotten up under him the way he had taught her and made it difficult.

Baby could feel his neck stiffen as she applied more pressure. She used her forearm to tighten her grip and wrapped her legs around his mid. She had waited patiently for the day to get him back for when he had applied the same maneuver on her down at the beach. And now, she was enjoying every moment of it. She kept her grip locked, but she could feel Treacherous getting stronger and didn't know how much longer she could hold him.

Treacherous dropped to his knees. Then, all in one motion, he forcefully pushed himself up. Baby held on with all her might and rode him like a bronco. Treacherous tried to reach behind himself to grab hold of her, but to no avail. Baby now had him in a full sleeper hold. Just as she thought she was going to subdue him, Treacherous pulled a rabbit out of the hat.

Baby grunted and released her grip from around Treacherous's neck. On impact, her back slammed up against the wall, knocking the wind out of her. She went crashing to the floor. Treacherous put his hands on his knees and looked back.

"You crazy, you know that?" he said, somewhat gasping for air.

"Like a fox." Baby smiled.

"I guess we're even." He returned her smile.

"Yup." Baby blew Treacherous a kiss and stuck her tongue out at him.

Treacherous grabbed hold of Baby's ankles and pulled her toward him. All of the play fighting had turned him on. He stared Baby in the eyes as he slid off her shorts and kneeled between her legs. Still looking up at her, he kissed the top of her cave and let his tongue brush against her clit. He could see Baby's chest rise and fall from the sensation his mouth caused. He smirked as he continued to plant light kisses and suck between Baby's inner thighs. He followed up with licks to each of her lips. Each stroke of his tongue caused Baby's body to quiver. Treacherous had learned her body very well and knew she loved getting head. He tenderly spread her lips and gently licked in between and round them before he moved in and teased her clit. He slid his hands underneath Baby's ass while he continued to lick around her inner thighs in slow, circular motions. Baby's body became one with the motion of Treacherous's tongue. She arched her back and moaned as she bit into her top lip and fondled her breasts through her wife beater.

Treacherous thrust her ass upward as he face and finger fucked Baby vigorously. He could feel her juices oozing down his chin as he attacked her clit with a stiff tongue and probed her box with his large middle finger. He continued his oral assault until he heard her gasping for air. Baby whispered his name through broken breaths.

She squirmed upward and tried to break away from him, but Treacherous had a firm lock on her ass cheeks. Baby tried to control her breathing, but Treacherous made it very hard to do. She felt his thumb slide the hood of her clitoris back, as two fingers dug deeper into her wetness. The surprise attack sent Baby over the edge. Her mouth hung open in ecstasy as her body braced for the storm that followed. Baby's toes curled as a wave made its way from the back of her neck down to her thighs. Her entire body twisted like a pretzel. Baby pushed Treacherous's head from between her legs and arched her back like the Golden Gate Bridge. Treacherous sat there smiling.

"You make me sick, boy," she said in between deep breaths. "That shit was serious."

Treacherous tried to rise, but Baby pushed him to the floor and onto his back. Then, she climbed on top of him. She kissed him deeply.

"I love the way you make my body feel." Baby looked deeply into Treacherous's eyes.

"Yeah?" Treacherous grinned.

"Tsk." Baby sucked her teeth. "Yeah, punk ass."

She tried to reach between Treacherous's legs, but he grabbed her hand.

"Get your horny ass up. We got work to do." Treacherous laughed.

He knew he had turned Baby on the way she turned him. He also knew if he let her stay on top of him any longer nothing would have gotten accomplished that day, nothing they had planned anyway.

"Now, we're even." He smiled and lifted Baby off of him.

"Fuck you," Baby playfully cursed.

Treacherous shook his head and didn't feed into the trap he knew Baby was trying to lure him into.

"This is it. You ready?" Treacherous became serious.

"Ready as I'll ever be," Baby replied, matching his tone. She knew what he was referring to. At first, she was skeptical about sharing her thoughts with Treacherous on the matter, but, after he had disclosed to her what would make him sleep better at night, she revealed what would bring her more comfort at night as well. That was weeks ago. Since then, Baby had been waiting for this day to come. She had dreamed about this moment countless of times, and now, thanks to Treacherous, it would soon be a reality.

"I'm about to jump in the shower, so we can go see what's good at that spot we been checkin' out. You gettin' in'?" Treacherous asked as he stood up.

"Yeah, I'll be in there," she replied.

Treacherous slipped out of his boxer briefs and snatched up his towel off the edge of the door. Then, he headed for the bathroom.

"If they strapped the way you think they are, this could be the one for us," Treacherous said, sounding hopeful.

Ever since Baby had told him about the place she used to hear her father talk about there was nothing else Treacherous could think about more than the final phase of their plan. He knew they weren't ready to take down a bank or an armored car yet like his parents or grandfather, but the small establishment Baby spoke of seemed like a walk in the park compared to the other capers they had pulled off. Their last score had put them back on their feet and had maintained a roof over their heads, but Treacherous was looking for the big payday to put them over the top. He was tired of Richmond and was ready to get Baby up out of her hometown and go back across the water to the Seven Cities where he was from. He was eager to show her that he could take care of them and hold it down no matter what. She had shown, on more than one occasion, how much and how hard she would ride for him. He felt it was only right to show her that it had all been worth it and believed the only way to do that was by getting that money. Besides, with all the dead bodies they had left behind, he was sure it was just a matter of time before the Richmond authorities got on their trail if they weren't already.

"Since I was a kid, I've heard stories about how that place is just a front for money laundering and a whole bunch of other stuff," Baby told him. "Don't worry. If it's not, then we'll just find something else to hit. Either way, we're gonna be okay." She smiled.

"You're right," Treacherous agreed. "I just wanna get this done and get the hell outta Richmond before it's too late," he added.

Baby nodded her head in agreement.

"Anyway," Treacherous said, changing the subject, "I'm gonna hop in. Don't be takin' too long," he warned.

Baby shot him the middle finger and smiled sarcastically.

Treacherous shook his head. He wasn't surprised by her comeback. "I love you too," he retorted.

Then, he turned on the shower.

Chapter 35

On what seemed like the hundredth ring, Detective Love answered his phone. He was met with a blaring shout in his ear.

"Who the hell is this?" he cursed.

The roar of his voice woke his wife.

"Art, it's me. Randle."

Detective Love immediately became alert. "Talk to me. What's up?" He flung the covers off his body and climbed out of bed.

"Honey, what's wrong?" a sleepy Jazmyne Love asked, looking over her shoulder.

"Nothing, sweetheart. Go back to bed," he whispered. Then, he tiptoed out of his bedroom.

"I just got word from a friend of mine that a couple fitting the description of my boy and your daughter took down a spot down on Broad Street that was under surveillance by the big boys. I heard it's pretty messy down there. A couple of ours got tagged."

"What? Are you kidding me?" Detective Love couldn't believe his ears.

"If I'm lying, I'm dying," Andre Randle replied. "I'm on my way down there right now."

"What's the place?"

"I don't know the name of it. I just know it was supposed to be a front for illegal monies for some heavy hitters."

"Holy fuck! I know exactly what place you're talking about. I'll meet you there."

Detective Love grabbed his forehead. After receiving the disturbing news, there was no doubt in his mind that his daughter was in over her head and was unable to be saved. The question now was whether her fate would be death or prison. With that being his thought, Detective Love hurried to get dressed and then was out the door.

Chapter 36

The sound of the chimes over Black's Pawnshop entrance alerted fifty-eight-year-old Sammy Black of someone's presence. A smile appeared across his pale white face at the sight of the beautiful specimen. He ran his fingers through his red and gray hair, making sure it was lying just the way he liked it.

"How may I be of service to you, pretty, young lady?" he asked, throwing in a compliment. You couldn't tell Sammy Black that he wasn't a ladies' man. Although he was as Irish as they came, he had a fetish for black women, specifically young ones. *Today must be my lucky day,* he thought.

"I would like to know if you have any nice digital cameras."

"Why, yes, my dear. I most certainly do." Sammy Black beamed, flashing his perfectly whitened piano keys. "If you'll just walk with me over to this side," he instructed her with the extension of his arm.

"Is this for school purposes or just for leisure?" he asked, pulling the keys out of his pocket to unlock the display case.

Just then, the chimes echoed in the air once again, informing Sammy Black of the male customer who had just walked through the door.

"I'll be with you in just a moment, young man," Sammy said toward the doorway. Then, he bent over to unlock the display case. "Here we go."

Sammy was stopped short of his sentence when he looked up to find two guns staring him in the face. He snickered.

"Come on, you kids. Don't be stupid," Sammy Black calmly tried to reason. He wasn't the least bit afraid.

"Shut the fuck up, old man!" Treacherous barked. "This ain't no fuckin' game."

Treacherous walked over to Sammy Black and smacked him across the face with the barrel of his gun. The blow didn't knock him out, but it was strong enough to send Sammy Black's boxer frame slamming up against the wall.

"You fuckin' piece of shit." Sammy Black spit out the blood that filled his mouth complimentary of the assault Treacherous had just delivered. "You think you and your bitch can just come in here and push me the hell around and try to take what's mine, huh? You must be out of your fucking mind!" Sammy Black bellowed. "Do you know who the fuck I am?"

"I know who the fuck you were."

The shot from Baby's gun ripped through Sammy Black's skull and killed him instantly. Treacherous wasted no time rushing to the door which led to the back of the pawnshop. He jiggled the handle only to find that it was locked. All in one motion, Treacherous used all his strength to kick the door off its hinges, while Baby locked the front door and posted up.

It took all of Treacherous's willpower to keep his composure. His and Baby's timing couldn't have been more perfect. He was convinced that the bags sitting on the round table were a gift from the Creator. Treacherous unraveled the string from around one of the bags and looked inside. He smiled at the stacks of money it contained. Treacherous wasted no time pulling out the folded up duffle bag from out of his pants. He threw the bag on the floor. Rather than load the duffle bag up with the bags on the table, Treacherous snatched up the tablecloth and wrapped it up. He then stuffed the entire bundle into the duffle bag, zipped it up, and tossed it over his shoulder.

When he returned to the front part of the pawnshop, he saw that Baby was still posted up by the entrance, holding down the fort.

"How we lookin' out there?" he asked.

"Everything looks good. No real traffic's come by at all." She looked out the window as she spoke. She turned around when she was done. Baby saw the large bulky duffle bag and smiled.

"I told you it would be a piece of cake," she gloated.

"Once again, you were right, babe." Treacherous kissed her on the lips.

"Where'd you park after you let me out?" Baby asked.

"Right on the side of the building."

"Okay. Let's get out of here."

Baby unlocked the front door of the pawnshop. Rather than tuck her gun, she kept it out and down at her side as an extra precaution. Because of the size of the bag Treacherous was carrying, she didn't want to take any chances on them getting jacked. The area they were in on Broad Street was known for being pretty rough territory, so she didn't put anything past anyone.

Baby opened the door and stepped out. She looked to the left and to the right. "Clear," she announced. She held the door open for Treacherous, who also had his gun down at his side, just in case.

Because of how smoothly things were going, he doubted he would have to use it. That doubt was quickly removed when the voice of someone came out of nowhere.

"Freeze, assholes," were the words that accompanied a barrage of bullets, coming from the direction of a black van that two men hopped out of the back of. A gunfight erupted as Treacherous and Baby returned fire.

Treacherous dropped the bag from his shoulder and took cover behind the car parked outside the pawnshop, while Baby opted for the tree off to the left. Treacherous quickly pulled out another clip from his pocket to replace the empty sixteen-shot clip he had just unloaded on the unexpected men, while Baby did the same with the speed loader with her revolver. Once the gun was reloaded, Treacherous rose up. What he saw pleased him. Both men were down on the ground. He got Baby's attention and pointed. Then, he walked around the car.

The two men lay bleeding. One of the agents bled profusely from the neck while the other had his hand pressed tightly against his lower abdomen. Treacherous peered into the back of the open van doors. The high-tech equipment inside confirmed what Treacherous had thought. He knew there was no turning back now. When he turned, Baby was picking up the second gun belonging to the two men on the ground, who lay fighting for their lives. Without saying anything, Treacherous stood over the cop closest to him and pumped four shots into the man's face and two more just below his bulletproof vest. Baby wasted no time doing the same to the other officer.

"Let's get the fuck out of here and handle what we gotta do before it's too late," Treacherous stated.

"Right behind you, babe."

Treacherous didn't have to tell her what he saw in the back of the van, just like he didn't have to tell her what their next move was.

Chapter 37

"Don't worry about it. It's on me."

Andre Randle picked up the check and viewed the total. He dug into his pocket and retrieved forty dollars, which was more than enough to cover the dinner bill.

"Thanks," Detective Love replied. "The next one's on me."

"Any dessert for you guys?" Judy, the waitress, asked, smiling.

"None for me." Andre Randle was the first to answer.

"Me neither." The two men rubbed their bellies, indicating how full they were.

"Okay. I'll be right back with your change."

Andre waved his hand. "No change."

Judy smiled again. "Thank you. You guys have a wonderful day."

Both Andre and Detective Love got up and stretched. "Been a hell of a day," Detective Love said and shook his head.

"Pretty much," Andre Randle agreed.

He empathized with what Detective Love was going through. His reasons for getting involved were personal, but they, in no way, compared to the detective's personal connection. The hurt in his eyes as he spoke about his daughter told the story of a father's pain. He could only imagine how difficult it was for him to assist in a manhunt where his child was the one being hunted.

"I'm really sorry about your kid getting all wrapped up in this mess," Andre Randle offered. "I'll give you a buzz if I find out anything worthwhile."

"Thanks, Randle."

The two men gave each other nods and hopped into their vehicles. Andre Randle backed out of the parking space. The sound of Detective Love's horn blowing wildly stopped him in his tracks. He threw his car into park. Then, he instinctively drew his gun and hopped out of his vehicle. He crouched down and scurried over to Chief Randle's unmarked car. Within seconds, he was pointing his gun back and forth from the front passenger window to the back. When he looked, he was confused but relieved to see that Detective Love was in no danger. He noticed Detective Love was motioning for him to get in the car.

"Sweetheart, don't worry, I'm on my way," were the words Andre Randle was met with when he opened the car door.

Detective Love discontinued the call. "Fuck!" he cursed. "Fuck! Fuck! Fuck!" Detective Love banged his fists on the steering wheel.

"Art, what the hell is going on?" Andre Randle asked.

"They got my fuckin' wife."

"Who?" Andre Randle became wide-eyed.

"My goddamn daughter and that motherfucker!"

"Holy shit!" Andre Randle now joined the detective in swearing.

"Jesus!" Detective Love dropped his head onto the steering wheel. "I can't believe this is happening. Not my baby girl."

"Art, it happens, man. It's nothing you did," a sympathetic Andre Randle said, trying to console the detective. "And that's not the little girl you remember. She's changed. The main thing now is to be strong for your wife. Where are they?"

Detective Love raised his head and wiped his eyes. He said, "You're absolutely right. She's not. I knew that, just didn't want to admit it." Detective Love let out a deep sigh. After pulling himself together, he answered, "They're at my house."

"Are you going to call it in?"

"No."

"I didn't think so," Andre Randle stated. "Well, I'm going with you," he said.

"No; she said that they told me to come alone."

"Fuck them. They don't call the shots or make the rules, we do," Andre Randle pointed out. "If you go there by yourself, both you and your wife are dead. These kids aren't playing. They've killed with no remorse or regard. I mean, come on, you know who this kid's parents were. It's almost as if he and your daughter are his parents reincarnated or something. I'm not letting you go by yourself."

Detective Love knew Randle was right. "Okay, but stay out of sight. I don't want to do anything that would give them a reason to hurt my wife. I'm going to text you my address."

"You got it," Andre Randle assured him before reaching for the door handle.

"And one more thing." Detective Love paused. "If you have to, do what you gotta do," he added.

Andre Randle knew what he meant. He gave a knowing nod. Then, he exited the detective's vehicle.

Chapter 38

Arthur Love slowly opened the front door of his home and entered with caution. Aside from the light he could see coming from the kitchen area, the inside of his home was dark. There was complete silence. It was so quiet that he could hear his own heart beating through his shirt at a faster pace than normal. His senses were on high alert, and he was ready for whatever.

With his weapon drawn, Arthur Love maneuvered through the living room like a lion hunting its prey and made his way toward the kitchen. With each move, he secured the perimeter by flashing his gun in all areas of the house. He stopped short and put his back up against the wall when he reached the entrance of the kitchen. He carefully leaned his head forward to get a view of the scene in the kitchen. He snatched his head back at the sight.

"Shit!" he cursed under his breath. His mind was racing as he weighed his options. Before he could make up his mind, it was made for him.

"Dad, if you don't come in here, I'm going to kill her," the familiar voice echoed in the air.

Arthur Love exhaled. Then, he did as he was told.

Seeing his wife in the nude, gagged and tied to the kitchen chair, pierced Arthur Love's heart. He could see that she had been beaten. Her tearstained eyes were black and blue while her lips were swollen and revealed traces of blood in the creases of her mouth. The blood on the side of her head had dried up and matted down a chunk of her hair.

"You did this?" His voice cracked as he addressed his daughter.

"Well, it's good to see you too, Daddy," Baby offered instead.

Treacherous was posted up against the wall with his .45 automatic zeroed in on Baby's father. Arthur Love cut his eyes over in Treacherous's direction and saw the weapon pointed at him. His blood boiled.

"Honey, are you all right?" he asked his wife.

Jazmyne Love nodded.

"Aw, he wants to know if you're okay!" Baby mocked in disgust.

"Baby girl, what are you doing?" Arthur Love asked his daughter. His tone was compassionate.

"Don't fuckin' call me that," Baby spat. "You gave up the right to call me that when you let them muthafuckas put me away."

Her words tore into her father as if they were hot slugs from her gun. It was the first time she had ever expressed how she felt about the outcome to him.

"Put you away? Sweetheart, you killed your aunt," Arthur Love pointed out. "It was either there or prison and I didn't want—"

Treacherous couldn't help but laugh.

"Fuck you. You piece of shit!" Arthur Love lashed out at Treacherous.

"No! Fuck you, nigga!" Treacherous's cocked his gun and lined it up with Arthur's head. "You don't know shit about your daughter," he barked.

"And I guess you do," Arthur Love retorted, pointing his own gun at Treacherous. He was not the least bit afraid. "She wasn't raised like you. She knows who her parents are, and we're not fucking killers!" he shouted.

Treacherous's finger applied pressure to the trigger of his gun.

"Treach! Please! No!" Baby pleaded. She knew he was about to pull the trigger. "Daddy, shut up!" she called out to her father. "Treach, stay out of this! I got it," she told him.

Treacherous lowered his gun. When Arthur Love turned around, he was met with his daughter's own gun now pointing at him.

"So, now you're going to shoot me? You're gonna shoot your father?"

"No," Baby quickly replied. "I mean, don't give me a reason to."

"Baby, what is all of this? This is not you." Arthur Love sighed. "You're runnin' around with this joker, robbing and killing people like it's legal. And now this?" He pointed to her mother. "You don't come from all of this. That's not how you were raised. What happened to you? What happened to my baby girl?"

Tears began to build up in Arthur Love's eyes, while a murderous grin appeared across Baby's face. She shook her head in pity. She couldn't believe how naïve he was about everything.

"Baby, please tell me, what happened to my little girl?" he begged Baby through sobs.

"You were supposed to protect me!" she blurted out. Baby could no longer fight the inevitable. She was now crying uncontrollably. "You were supposed to protect me! Goddamn it!"

"From what, honey?" Arthur Love tried to move in to console his daughter.

"Don't! Stay the fuck where you are," she warned as she waved her gun.

"Okay! Take it easy." Arthur Love paused in his tracks and threw his hands up. "What happened? What didn't I protect you from?"

Baby let out a sinister laugh. She drew her attention to her mother, who had been listening and watching with keen ears and fearful eyes.

"Why don't you ask your fuckin' wife?" Baby snatched the gag from her mother's mouth.

Arthur Love stood confused.

"Ask her!" Baby screamed.

"Honey?" Arthur Love shifted his eyes to his wife. "What's going on?"

"I'm s . . . sorry." Jazmyne Love dropped her head and began to sob.

"No, bitch! Look at him and tell him what you're sorry about." Baby went behind her mother and grabbed hold of her head. She raised it up and yelled, "Tell him!" Baby cocked the hammer of her gun and pressed the barrel up against the back of her mother's head.

"Okay!" her mother yelled out. Jazmyne closed her eyes and took a deep breath. She relived the scene that had been haunting her for years. She shook her head and cleared her throat. "Baby didn't mean to kill Jazelle. Everything happened so fast."

"What? What are saying, Jazmyne? What was happening so fast?" Arthur Love wanted to know. He had never been so confused in his life.

"Let her finish," Baby interjected. "Finish," she told her mother.

"Jazelle should have never been killed." She paused. "She was trying to protect me," Jazmyne cried out. "It was me she was trying to kill!"

"What the hell are you talking about?" Arthur Love could not comprehend what his wife was saying. Nothing was making sense to him.

"You heard what she said," Baby chimed in. "I was trying to kill her ass, not Aunt Jazelle."

"But why, Baby?"

Baby poked her mother in the back of her head with the weapon. "Tell him why, Jazmyne," she said, refusing to call her Mother.

"I was wrong. I was wrong," Jazmyne repeated.

"Fuck all of that!" Baby smacked her mother across the face with side of her gun. "Bitch, you got two seconds to tell your muthafuckin' husband why your funky ass convinced him to put me away."

"Baby." Jazmyne sighed in a low tone.

It was the first time Baby had heard her mother say her name since they had been there. Her voice and the way she said it triggered something inside Baby.

"I remember when you used to say my name like that." Baby leaned over. "Remember this!" she whispered in her mother's ear. Baby took her gun and shoved it between her mother's legs. The barrel of her weapon penetrated her mother. Jazmyne screamed in agony.

"Baby, that's enough!"

Arthur Love had his gun locked on his daughter's head. He was tempted to take the shot, but his mind was changed by the barrel that Treacherous had pressed up against his temple.

"I wish you would, mu'fucka," Treacherous threatened Baby's father in the most chilling tone known to mankind.

Baby didn't bother turning around. There was no doubt in her mind that Treacherous had her back. Instead, she concentrated on her mother.

"You like that?" Baby asked as she slid her gun in and out of her mother's vagina.

"Baby, please don't," her mother cried.

"'Just one of those days,'" Baby began to sing.

Tears flowed profusely out of Jazmyne Love's eyes.

"Baby, I'm begging you," Arthur Love tried to reason with his daughter. "Whatever it is or whatever it was, I'm sorry I wasn't there for you, but I'm here now," he added.

His words had melted a layer of Baby's hardened heart, but there were ninety-nine more that he had no way of knowing he hadn't been able to reach.

"It's too late," Baby said calmly.

She removed her gun from her mother's vagina and stood up. The combination of her mother's fluids and blood dripped from the barrel. Baby stared menacingly at her mother.

"I hope wherever you're going you're forgiven for what you did to me because I never will," Baby said as she walked behind her mother.

"Daddy, I'm sorry," she said just before she squeezed the trigger.

"No! Jaz!"

"No! Baby!"

The sound of gunshots filled the Loves' residence. The first shot that triggered the barrage of bullets whizzing through the air exited Baby's gun and ended Jazmyne Love's defenseless life on impact. Simultaneously, the first of two shots from Andre Randle's gun shattered the kitchen window's glass and wildly spiraled its way into the refrigerator. The third shot that followed was intended for Baby, but it ripped through Treacherous's upper torso and almost forced him off his feet. As the shot was fired, he had made a mad dash over to her and posed as a human shield.

The three shots Treacherous managed to get off in the direction of the window before he was hit made their presence felt. The first one grazed Andre Randle's left cheek while the second one tore into his shoulder and knocked him off the milk crate he stood on outside. The third one ricocheted off Arthur Love's gun and lodged itself in the kitchen's wall. Arthur Love never got a chance to get off a shot. The bullet from Treacherous's gun sent his weapon flying across the room.

"Treach," Baby screamed. She immediately rushed to Treacherous's side and fell to the floor. At that moment, nothing mattered but her man. She was oblivious to everything else.

"Treach! Wake up, babe!" Baby rubbed his face.

Treacherous lay dead still. Blood gushed from his body, staining his shirt.

"No! You can't leave me," Baby cried. She pressed her head up against Treacherous's face. "Treach, please wake up."

The room felt as if it were spinning to Baby. *This was not the plan,* she thought. The last thing she would have ever imagined was something happening to her partner. She could not fathom life without Treacherous. For her, it was not an option. Baby pulled herself together. She knew what she had to do.

"Don't worry, babe. I'm going to get you outta here." She kissed Treacherous on the cheek. Just as she stood up, she heard her name. When she looked, her father was aiming his gun at her.

"How could you do this to me?" Arthur Love tightened his grip on his gun.

"To you?" Baby was surprised by his statement.

"How could you kill your mother?" he asked.

"That molesting-ass bitch killed your daughter a long time ago. Now, we're even," Baby slyly remarked.

"Don't you fucking talk about her like that," he shouted.

"You don't even care what she did to me!" Baby shot daggers at her father. "You're no different than her!"

"Go to hell!" Arthur Love cursed.

"Eventually," Baby mocked. "And I'll tell Jazmyne you said hi when I get there." Baby kneeled down and got behind Treacherous's body.

"I can't let you leave here."

"Well, then, you're going to have to kill me because I'm taking my man up out of here," she retorted.

"Damn it, Baby. Don't make me do this."

Baby kept both her eyes and her gun on her father while she lifted Treacherous up.

Arthur Love cocked his weapon. "Baby, I'm warning you."

It was if as though his words had fallen on deaf ears. Baby continued to drag Treacherous's body out of the kitchen and toward the living room area. Her father followed her as she slowly made her way into the living room. Baby knew he was torn between his duty as an officer and his love for her. She used that to her advantage. Baby finally reached the door.

"Don't you open that door," Arthur Love warned his daughter.

Unfazed by his words, Baby reached back and grabbed the door handle.

"I told you not to open that fucking door!" Arthur Love's gun roared like the king of the jungle. The bullet spun Baby around and sent her crashing to the floor. It was not Arthur Love's intention to kill his daughter but rather wound her. He could have easily put a bullet through her heart, which he was tempted to do, but, instead, he opted for her left arm.

"Muthafucka!"

Baby wasted no time retaliating. She let off four shots in succession in the direction of her father. Arthur Love dove for cover just in time to escape two of the bullets that would have surely found permanent homes in his body. He was not so lucky to dodge the third and fourth shots though. The first one burned into the back of his right calf while the other ripped through his ribcage. He could feel the blood oozing from his side. The burning sensation that started in his calf muscle steadily made its way through his entire body. Arthur Love positioned himself against the back of his living room sofa out of harm's way. He slid his leg over, which had become numb. Then, he pressed his hand up against his side.

The shots fired at her father made for a great diversion for Baby. They were able to provide her with enough time to regain her balance. She raised herself from the floor. Then, with all her strength, she lifted Treacherous's body again.

"I'm getting you out of here." She threw Treacherous's arm around her neck and opened the door.

"Baby!" Arthur Love yelled out his daughter's name.

Baby never bothered to turn around. She continued to drag both herself and Treacherous out the door.

"Shit!" Arthur Love cursed.

He closed his eyes tightly and banged his head repeatedly on the back of the couch. His chest heaved uncontrollably. He knew what he had to do.

"Baby!" He peeked around the sofa and yelled out again.

He saw that his daughter had made her way out the door. A tear rolled down Arthur Love's face as he released three more shots through the open door at his fleeing daughter right before he lost consciousness.

Chapter 39

Baby drove aimlessly with no destination in mind. Her arm was sore from the gunshot wound inflicted by her father and she was tired. She had ditched the previous getaway car and hotwired another one. She knew it was just a matter of time before they'd be looking for the BMW they had fled her old home in. Being the daughter of a cop, she was trained in the way police thought, so she also knew she had to stay off the main roads and highways for now.

The empty, pitch dark back road she traveled on only added to the drowsiness that continued to fall upon her though. The blaring of the music coming from the stereo system did little to help, so Baby shut it off. It was her survival instincts that kept her wide-eyed and alerted her each time she dozed and swerved. Every other minute, she looked over at Treacherous, who was still unconscious. Her heart ached each time she looked at his still body. She shook off the guilt that tried to creep in, knowing that, if the shoe were on the other foot, she would have done the same for him. She knew it was because of her Treacherous was in the condition he was in. Had it not been for him trying to protect her, she may have not been alive, and she was grateful for that.

All she could think about was losing him. She knew if she didn't get him medical attention soon that may very well be the case. The thought made Baby think about not wanting to live anymore herself. The scene reminded her of one Treacherous had read to her about his parents. As tears escaped from Baby's burning eyes, she reached over and rubbed the side of his face.

"Just hold on, babe," she pleaded.

Baby saw the sign she was looking for that read three miles to the interstate.

"Don't you fuckin' leave me, Treacherous," Baby cried. "We got shit to do."

"I ain't goin' nowhere." The words were low and raspy but loud enough for Baby to hear them.

She nearly lost control of the wheel. When she looked over, Treacherous was staring at her with his signature smile partially revealed across his face.

"Boy, you scared the shit out of me." Baby smiled as the tears streamed down her face. "I thought I was gonna lose you." She leaned over and kissed Treacherous. Then, she rubbed and massaged the back of his head and neck. "I got to get you to a doctor."

"I s . . . saw—"

Baby cut him off before he could finish. She saw the interstate sign up ahead. "Shhh. Save your strength, babe. I'm going to figure this out." She seemed hopeful.

"Babe, listen." Treacherous used what little strength he had to raise his hand and placed it on Baby's lap. Baby was now all ears.

"I saw him."

"Saw who, babe?" Baby thought he was delusional from the bullets he had taken. She placed her hand on top of his.

"The mu'fucka who killed my mother!" Treacherous's tone hardened.

"What? Where?" a confused Baby asked.

"At the house."

It all made sense to Baby now. She instantly regretted not searching outside the house for the shooter who had caught them by surprise. She knew time was not on her side though and chose securing her and Treacherous's safety over retaliation. Besides, there was no way of knowing that the man they intended to find and kill next was right up under their very noses.

"I can't believe this shit," Baby cursed.

She was tempted to turn around and go back but knew the house would be crawling with cops by then. Instead, she merged on to I-95 North.

"We didn't know," Treacherous told her.

He was just as surprised to see the face of the man who had been haunting him for the past five years. Luckily, he had detected the movement outside the window before the man was able to take another woman he had loved away from him. The thought of that almost being the case set Treacherous on fire. At that moment, there was nothing else that would bring him more pleasure than taking the life of the man he remembered everybody refer to as Chief Randle.

Baby saw the disturbing look on her man's face. "Don't worry about it, babe. I promise we'll find him, and, when we do . . ." She let her words linger.

"It's over for him," Treacherous said, finishing her sentence.

Chapter 40

"How you feeling?" Arthur Love asked, rolling the wheelchair he was in alongside Andre Randle's bed.

"I'm alive." Andre Randle smiled.

"Same thing I said."

"Any news?"

"They found the car they were in. Other than that, they've checked all the hospitals and come up with nothing. My daughter's a smart girl and a survivor, so my guess is they're far away from this area by now."

"Yeah, I figured as much." Andre Randle shook his head. "How are you holding up?" he asked.

"Aside from the fact that my child killed my wife, made me a widower, and is a fugitive, I'm okay."

Andre Randle didn't know what to say.

"Thank you." Arthur Love put his hand on Andre Randle's shoulder.

"For what?"

"For trying."

"Wasn't good enough." Andre Randle grimaced.

Just then, the nurse popped her head in and interrupted the two men. "Sorry, guys, but it's time for the both of you to be seen by the doctor, so, Detective, I need you to make your way back to your room."

"Thank you, Nurse."

The nurse flashed a smile before she left the room.

"I'll see you later," Arthur Love announced. He spun his wheelchair around and headed toward the door.

"Art," Andre called out, "don't worry. If they don't catch them before we get out of here, we'll find them. I think I have a good idea where to look."

Arthur Love nodded his head. Then, he turned and wheeled himself out of Andre Randle's room.

Chapter 41

Big Lou knocked on his boss's office door before letting himself in. He walked over to the desk and handed him the cell phone.

"Boss, sorry to bother you, but I think you should take this call." The nervousness showed all over Big Lou's face.

"What the hell is wrong with you, and who's on the phone?" Big Lou's boss asked.

"It's Charlie from Richmond." Big Lou paused. "It's about your father."

The mention of his father alerted Big Lou's boss. The only time his old man didn't call him directly was when there was a problem.

"Yeah, Charlie. It's me. What's up?"

The items on Sammy Black Jr.'s desk nearly bounced off from the impact of his fist crashing down on it. "Who the fuck was it?" he boomed into the phone.

He couldn't believe someone had the heart to make a move on his family, unless they had a death wish. His father was a made guy, and their family was connected. Aside from that, Sammy Junior had established in the streets of Virginia before he relocated to Miami that if anyone messed with his family he wouldn't stop until he wiped out theirs. He was almost certain that it was not mob related for two reasons. One because it would be like stealing from themselves and two, none of the other families would risk bringing that type of heat on themselves unless they intended to try to take over. The questions now were who, why, and how was someone able to pull this off?

"What about the chips?" He knew the answer to his own question. He just needed to hear it for himself.

"I got a million fuckin' dollars cash for whoever brings me whoever is responsible for my father's death or leads me to the cocksuckers. You hear me, Charlie?" Sammy Junior fought the emotions that wanted to reveal how hurt he was. "And, I want them alive!" He knew the party responsible for the murder of his father and the heist of the merchandise left in his father's care was of no use to him dead. There was no way to bring his father back, but he knew if he didn't recover what was taken, he might very well end up being buried alongside his father.

Sammy Junior discontinued the call. Then, with all his might, he flung the cell phone at the wall like A-Rod pitching in a World Series game. The phone shattered into pieces on impact.

"Book us a flight to Richmond," he instructed Big Lou.

"On it, boss." Big Lou scurried out of the office and closed the door behind him.

When he was gone, Sammy Junior pulled out his own cell phone and scrolled through his contacts. He found who he was looking for and dialed the number. The caller picked up on the first ring.

"Yeah, I need you to meet me in Richmond in the morning. We have a family emergency."

That was all he needed to say. Sammy Junior hung up and placed his phone back on his hip. Then, he laid his head on his desk and wept for the loss of his father.

To be continued in *Ride Or Die Chick 4: Riders 4 Lyfe*

ORDER FORM
URBAN BOOKS, LLC
97 N18th Street
Wyandanch, NY 11798

Name (please print):_____

Address: _____

City/State: _____

Zip: _____

QTY	TITLES	PRICE
	16 On The Block	$14.95
	A Girl From Flint	$14.95
	A Pimp's Life	$14.95
	Baltimore Chronicles	$14.95
	Baltimore Chronicles 2	$14.95
	Betrayal	$14.95
	Bi-Curious	$14.95
	Bi-Curious 2: Life After Sadie	$14.95
	Bi-Curious 3: Trapped	$14.95
	Both Sides Of The Fence	$14.95
	Both Sides Of The Fence 2	$14.95
	California Connection	$14.95

Shipping and handling: add $3.50 for 1st book, then $1.75 for each additional book.

Please send a check payable to:

Urban Books, LLC

Please allow 4-6 weeks for delivery

ORDER FORM
URBAN BOOKS, LLC
97 N18th Street
Wyandanch, NY 11798

Name (please print):_____

Address: _____

City/State: _____

Zip: _____

QTY	TITLES	PRICE
	California Connection 2	$14.95
	Cheesecake And Teardrops	$14.95
	Congratulations	$14.95
	Crazy In Love	$14.95
	Cyber Case	$14.95
	Denim Diaries	$14.95
	Diary Of A Mad First Lady	$14.95
	Diary Of A Stalker	$14.95
	Diary Of A Street Diva	$14.95
	Diary Of A Young Girl	$14.95
	Dirty Money	$14.95
	Dirty To The Grave	$14.95

Shipping and handling: add $3.50 for 1st book, then $1.75 for each additional book.

Please send a check payable to:

Urban Books, LLC

Please allow 4-6 weeks for delivery

ORDER FORM
URBAN BOOKS, LLC
97 N18th Street
Wyandanch, NY 11798

Name (please print):_____

Address: _____

City/State: _____

Zip: _____

QTY	TITLES	PRICE
	Gunz And Roses	$14.95
	Happily Ever Now	$14.95
	Hell Has No Fury	$14.95
	Hush	$14.95
	If It Isn't love	$14.95
	Kiss Kiss Bang Bang	$14.95
	Last Breath	$14.95
	Little Black Girl Lost	$14.95
	Little Black Girl Lost 2	$14.95
	Little Black Girl Lost 3	$14.95
	Little Black Girl Lost 4	$14.95
	Little Black Girl Lost 5	$14.95

Shipping and handling: add $3.50 for 1st book, then $1.75 for each additional book.
Please send a check payable to:
Urban Books, LLC
Please allow 4-6 weeks for delivery